The Oklahoma Land Company

The Oklahoma Land Company

By

Danny W. Glidewell

Copyright © 2003 by Danny W. Glidewell.
Printed in the United States. All rights reserved.

ISBN: 1-58597-201-0

Library of Congress Control Number: 2003108805

A division of Squire Publishers, Inc.
4500 College Blvd.
Leawood, KS 66211
1/888/888-7696
www.leatherspublishing.com

To Madelyn

Chapter 1

J AKE SPOONHOUR PUSHED back from the table and stood with his hands holding his now full belly. "Woman," Jake moans, "you're going to kill me with food like that. I'm going to eat myself to death," he said with a sigh.

Jake and Jenny were married just three years before, but had known each other since they were kids growing up together back in the Smoky Hills of Tennessee. That was some ten years ago. Jenny's folks lived just a mile and a half up the road from the Spoonhour place.

"You go out and sit on the porch and I'll be out in a minute with some more coffee," Jenny said with a hint of satisfaction in her voice. The satisfaction of knowing her man was pleased with the meal she had prepared.

Jenny was an attractive woman. Not what you would call striking, but just plain pretty. She had a tall slim frame of which she carried proudly. Back home in Tennessee, Jenny worked the farm, right along beside her two brothers. Jenny's brothers couldn't outwork her doing the chores as hard as they may have tried. It just wasn't in Jenny to take second place at anything.

Jake and Jenny never thought of each other as sweethearts or anything like that while growing up. They were just always friends. Jake was five years older than Jenny, but they went to the same one-room school back in Cosby, Tennessee.

After attending school in Cosby, Jenny went back east to an all-girls school. A college education was a rare thing in those days, especially for a girl of a poor family from the hill country of Tennessee. She worked and paid her own way which was tough, but Jenny felt it was something she had to do. It was like a drive within, a thirst that had to be quenched. After four years away at school, Jenny went back to Cosby and took over teaching at the same one-room school which she and Jake had attended. The small town of Cosby was very fortunate to have her back.

When Jenny went away to school, Jake had gone off to find his fortune. He tried his hand at mining up Colorado way for awhile. Jake panned enough gold to eat and that was about it. Of course, he was always good with a rope and no one could outride him. So the natural thing for Jake to do was to work the cattle drives along the Jesse Chisholm Trail from Texas to Kansas.

Jake Spoonhour knew the Chisholm Trail as well as any man. Cattle had become so numerous in Texas during the Civil War that a market had to be found, and the nearest rail shipping point was Abilene, Kansas. Rumor has it that 10 million longhorn cattle were driven over the Trail between 1866 and 1890. Herds varied from 3,000 to 10,000 head. Those drives usually started in the spring at various points in Texas and made the way north at a pace of about five to 15 miles a day. There were actually two trails used to move cattle from Texas north. They were the Jesse Chisholm and the John Chisum Trails. The two trails were often confused, but they were actually named after two different men. Both trails ran north and south, but the John Chisum Trail was the more westerly of the two.

The Jesse Chisholm Trail ran from Caldwell, Kansas to Wichita, after crossing Oklahoma, but the cattle trail which was the old Chisholm Trail extended to Abilene, Kansas; that was before there was any thought of Dodge City, or the John Chisum Trail that ran into Dodge City, Kansas from western Texas.

As the first Kansas cowtowns became settled, some trail drives went only as far north as first Newton, then Wichita and finally Caldwell where, by 1879, the railroad had been extended to the south from Abilene. By then, overland cattle drives were outlawed in parts of Kansas for fear of a tick-born disease sometimes carried by the Texas cattle that could wipe out a local rancher's herd. The drovers and the railroad worked around the law by pushing cattle into huge holding pens that were set up south of Caldwell at the Oklahoma border. The drive technically ended at the border where shipment by rail began.

It was on one of these cattle drives that Jake discovered a piece of land. It was in the northern central part of "The Territory" when Jake went out one morning to get a deer for Cookie to fix up for supper. Jake topped out over a hill to find a valley thick with trees and a stream running the length of the valley which was about a mile long and a half mile wide. The meadows were about 100 acres each, with thick, knee-high grass.

Jake was so taken by the sight that lay before him, he stepped from his horse, sat down and just stared for the most part of an hour. Jake knew this was a place a man could live out his life and never want for anything.

About six months after Jake found the valley, he heard rumors about land the Government was going to give away down in the Oklahoma Territory. They said, "All ya gotta do is run for it and be the first to stake out your acreage and it's yours."

Jake signed up for the "Run of '89" in Enid and was set to go after the land of his dreams. Of course, there were about 600 to 800 other people with the same dream. The valley that Jake had found while on the cattle drive was some 25 miles to the southeast of the start line, which was just south of Enid. Jake was hoping that the hidden valley had stayed hidden and no one else would be "running" for the same piece of ground.

This particular land run, which was one of a half of a dozen to be started around 1889 would start a mile south of Enid and run east. The rules were simple: when the start was given, you raced to the land you wanted as fast as you could. The land that was to be given away was marked off and each person who signed up was given a map. The map gave a general idea what land was available. The valley Jake wanted was in the marked-off area, but just barely. It was at the very southeast corner of the marked-off land.

Of course, anytime there's a good deal like land to be given away, there were always those people who will try to get an advantage. The Army had been given the task of patrolling the marked-off land to keep people from getting an early start and claiming the best land. If the Army found anyone in the marked land, those people would be escorted from the area. Most of the people who entered the land too soon would try to avoid the Army patrol or put up a fight. Those people were shot. There was no tolerance for *"Sooners."*

Jake was thinking about this while sitting on the porch, waiting for Jenny to bring out the coffee. He was also thinking of all the hard work he had put into building this place up to what it is today. What it is, is a 640-acre ranch with some of the finest cattle to be raised in Oklahoma or Texas for that matter. Jake built it with his own sweat and blood and with the help of his hired man, Julio Sanchez.

Four or five years ago, Julio was half-dead when Jake found him in a canyon about a two-hour ride west of the valley. It seemed that Julio had a run-in with some Indians and didn't fare too well. He did manage to escape but not before they worked him over pretty good. After a month or so, Julio was almost as good as new. The incident left Julio with a bad leg, which caused him to limp a bit. The leg also gave Julio some trouble when it was going to rain.

Jake's thoughts came back to the present when he heard the screen door open. "Looks like Julio is right again, might get some rain tonight," Jake said as he gratefully accepted a cup from Jenny. "That leg of his predicts the weather pretty good," Jake offered as thunder rumbled off in the southwest.

"What would you do without Julio?" Jenny asked with a smile. "Julio is more like family than a hired hand, that's for sure," Jake admitted. "He thinks he owes me something for saving him from those Indians."

Jake and Jenny sat watching the show off in the distance put on by the lightning. After a while Jenny grew sleepy and said as much, "I think I'll go on up and get ready for bed," she said with a yawn.

Jake said, "I'll be along in a bit after I finish this cup of coffee"

Jenny had gone through the door and was halfway to the stairs when she heard another clap of thunder. This one sounded a little closer, she thought to herself. At that point all of the color left Jenny's face and her heart sank as she realized that was not thunder at all. It was a gunshot! Jenny yelled to Jake as she turned for the door. Jake didn't answer. Jenny yelled again. Again there was no reply.

By this time Jenny had reached the door and was through it. As she stepped out Julio ran up from the bunkhouse. Jake was slumped in his chair which was still slightly rocking.

Jenny and Julio reached Jake at the same time, and as they did the faint rhythm of horse hooves sounded in the distance. Jake had a hole in his chest about the size of a nickel. He was bleeding badly from the wound, and Julio immediately tried to stop the bleeding.

Jake had blacked out from the shock but was regaining consciousness a little. Jenny bent over Jake, saying. "You'll be all right." Jenny was saying the words as much for herself as for Jake. As Jenny bent over Jake, he tried to speak. Jenny placed her ear next to Jake's lips and strained to hear.

"Julio, let's see if we can get him inside," Jenny said as she picked up Jake's feet, while indicating with her head for Julio to lift Jake's body. Jenny and Julio managed somehow to get Jake into the parlor where they tried to make him as comfortable as possible. Julio had slowed the bleeding and dressed the wound. Jake was unconscious again but breathing a little easier.

"Ma'am," Julio asked, "what did he say?"

Jenny looked at Julio and said, "Julio, I need you to head for town and see if Doc Sherman will come out and, Julio, pack yourself a bed roll to take with you. Jake said to find Cam VanPelt."

Chapter 2

THE SMALL TOWN of Marshall began as a crossroads store on the land claim of Sylvan T. Rice. Mr. Rice made his first sale from the low half dugout building on July 25, 1889. A post office was established on March I, 1890, in a lean-to which was added on to the north side of Rice's store.

In 1894, the town of Marshall was moved to its present site, about one-quarter mile to the southwest of the Rice store. A number of other businesses were soon established such as: a livery stable, a saloon, a bank, a jail with the sheriff's office and a hotel. Soon a newspaper and a feed store were built.

It was a hot windy day in Marshall, not too much different from most August days in the "Oklahoma Territory." A group of men came out of Shotgun Sam's Saloon.

The saloon was named after its owner, Samuel "Shotgun" Simmons, who always carried a sawed-off shotgun cradled in one arm all day long. He even had that scattergun with him while waiting tables or serving behind the bar. Shotgun Sam had very little trouble in his saloon.

The group of men were cursing and laughing about something or someone, as they stepped on to the boardwalk from the saloon. They were led by William Corsey, or Will as he liked to be called. Most people that knew or knew of Corsey called him, "Bad Bill Corsey," but not to his face. Corsey was worse than bad, he was mean through and through. He was downright cruel and enjoyed being that way. Corsey was a big man. He stood six feet three inches tall and tipped the scales at about 200 pounds.

Will Corsey had lost count of how many men he had killed. The first man was his own father. Will was 15 years old at the time and got tired of his dad whipping him for getting into trouble in his hometown back in Missouri. Will was waiting in the shadows inside their barn when his father came in with the razor strap. Will shot his dad four times before his father hit the ground and once again when his father was lying on the barn floor.

Will had planned ahead by taking his father's guns, a 30-30 Winchester rifle, a double barrel shotgun and the Colt 45 he had used to kill his dad. Will saddled his father's horse, loaded on the guns, then stepped into the saddle and rode away. That was 25 years ago, and to Corsey's way of thinking it was the best thing he ever did.

Shortly after Will Corsey left his home, he hooked up with William C. Quantrill. On the 21st of August 1863, Corsey was part of a band of cold-blooded murdering rebels, some 300 to 400 in number, that attacked and burned most of Lawrence, Kansas. They entered the town between daylight and sunrise, and by nine o'clock the city of 3,000 inhabitants laid in ruins and 125 to 150 people were massacred.

Eyewitnesses reported after entering Lawrence, the raiders scattered about the place in squads, each squad having predetermined lists of what houses they should burn and what citizens they should murder.

Corsey, along with a large number of the invaders, rode rapidly down Massachusetts Street to the Eldridge House, shooting all men and boys as fast as they appeared in sight. The streets of Lawrence were made to run red with innocent blood that morning, and Corsey reveled in the work they were doing. This was the non-auspicious beginning of a life of murder and crime for William Corsey.

Now, William Corsey is known as a killer for hire in about a five-state area. He is wanted in at least two states for different crimes, mostly murder.

The other men in the group were the typical low-lifes that followed men like Corsey. Pat McGlass was next in line of the pecking order. McGlass, also a murderer, was a little bigger than Corsey and was probably a little smarter. He didn't kill just anyone. McGlass killed only the ones he was hired to kill or the ones he thought might benefit him in some way.

McGlass became acquainted with Corsey while he too rode with Quantrill on their murderous raid on Lawrence. He just recently hooked back up with Corsey after McGlass had been riding with Henry Starr and his gang.

Henry Star was the nephew of the notorious Sam Starr who was married to Belle Starr, the "outlaw queen." During his 32 years of crime, Henry Starr claimed to have robbed more banks than both the

James-Younger Gang and the Doolin-Dalton Gang put together. Henry started robbing banks on horseback in 1863 and ended up robbing his last in a car in 1921, a total of 21 banks in all.

Pat McGlass joined up with Henry while working cattle on a ranch near Nowata in Indian Territory. McGlass rode with Henry's gang into Kansas and on March 28, 1893, they robbed their first bank in Chaney, Kansas, then moved on to rob a bank in Bentonville, Arkansas.

McGlass decided to look for a new profession when U.S. Deputy Marshals Henry C. Dickey and Floyd Wilson were hot on the trail of the Henry Starr Gang near Nowata. In a shoot-out with the two marshals, Henry and McGlass almost lost their lives.

They narrowly escaped and headed west where McGlass stopped in Enid, Oklahoma Territory, and Henry Starr along with Kid Wilson made tracks for California. McGlass joined up with Corsey in Enid and later headed down to Covington, O.T., for a meeting with a man named Lester Hoch who was hiring gunmen.

Next was Jim Enos, a half Mexican, known as a coward and a back shooter. Enos, very small in stature, was a chronic whiner. Corsey almost killed Jim one day just to shut him up and would have if McGlass had not stepped in and calmed Bad Bill down.

Enos also met Corsey while riding with Quantrill. Most recently he spent time in jail for participating in an attempted train robbery near Round Pond Station, north of Enid. Riding the train from Caldwell, Enos was to make his play from the inside after his partners in the crime, John T. O'Conners, Frank Lacey and Nate Sylva, stopped the train. Enos lost his nerve when railroad detective at that time and later to become a U.S. Marshal, W.D. "Bill" Fossett, noticed Jim, who was acting nervous and began questioning him.

After the holdup went bad, Fossett arrested Jim Enos but couldn't retain him for long because he really didn't do anything but act nervous. After his release, Enos headed down to Enid where he also hooked up with Corsey.

The fourth man in the group was Tom McKay. McKay was also a huge man, even bigger than Corsey or McGlass. McKay may have been the most dangerous of the bunch. The most dangerous mainly because you never knew what he was thinking.

Also a former Quantrill raider, McKay was very quiet and never spoke much unless it was to answer a question, and then it was a yes or no. Tom McKay was a cold-blooded killer, a lot like Corsey and maybe that's why they tolerated each other, kind of a mutual respect among killers.

Tom McKay, always a loner, preferred to work alone. He was wanted in Missouri for numerous murders. McKay would kill a person with very little warning, for whatever the man might have in his pockets. He killed two deputy sheriffs in Fort Smith, Arkansas, when the lawmen told McKay to reach for the sky and he reached for his gun instead. A shoot-out ensued, but the two deputies were no match for McKay's talent with a gun.

Corsey sent word to Tom McKay about joining him for a job, and Tom was soon on his way to Enid.

The last man in the group would probably be the last man in any group. Dave Kinsel was scum. He had the mentality of a rock; he was an idiot. Kinsel wasn't smart enough to know the difference between right and wrong, whereas Corsey knew the difference; he just didn't care.

Kinsel was a tagalong and had been following Will Corsey around picking up Will's leftovers and being his go-fer for a few months now.

As the five men strolled out of the saloon onto the boardwalk, there was an Indian sitting on the walk, leaning up against the front wall of the saloon to the right side of the door. He had an old leather hat that was pulled down low over his eye.

Corsey looked down in disgust. "I'd just as soon shoot those damned Indians as look at 'um," he cursed. As he spoke, he kicked the Indian's moccasin feet. "Damn drunken redskin," he growled. The Indian didn't move or acknowledge the kick.

The group went on laughing and cursing for five or six steps. All of a sudden Corsey stopped. He felt a cold chill run down his back. Something like he had never experienced before, like someone had walked on his grave. Corsey slowly turned to look back; the Indian was gone. Corsey and the rest started walking again. Corsey glanced back over his shoulder with a quizzical look on his face and kept walking.

"What's goin' on?" asked McGlass.

"Shut up," Corsey blurted.

Corsey didn't understand this feeling he had, and anytime he didn't understand something, he didn't like it.

The five turned down the alley between Shotgun Simmons and the next row of buildings, then went along the back of the stores to the east. The building at the end of the row was a survey office on the ground floor with more office space upstairs. Lester M. Hoch owned the building and occupied the top floor where he ran his many dealings that had made him a very wealthy man.

Lester Hoch was the largest landowner in the area. He had been buying up homesteads right and left for the last few years, using various land companies as a front. The land companies would give homesteaders who couldn't make a go of it ten cents on the dollar or less for their land,

These homesteaders had bigger dreams than they had know-how or work ethics. When most of the people came to run for the land, they were broke already. These people had no idea it would take time for the land to produce enough to live off. Lester Hoch was there with his vast wealth and took advantage of the homesteaders, but in a way it also helped a little. At least they got something for their land, enough sometimes to get their families back east to relatives.

It wasn't until all the easy buy-outs were made and people that wanted out had sold that Lester became greedy. He decided he wanted more, much more.

Hoch began to have some of his less scrupulous cowhands cause problems for some of the settlers that weren't ready to sell, problems like contaminated water holes and grass fires that would burn up the good grazing land. Lester also owned the only general store in town, although no one knew that he was the owner. Hoch had purchased the mortgage when old Burt Bass couldn't meet his payment. Hoch let Bass continue to run the store for him, if Burt would keep his mouth shut and not tell anyone who really owned the place. Hoch instructed Burt Bass not to extend any more credit to certain settlers. Without supplies the settlers couldn't survive until their crops came in. Things didn't get real bad until Hoch brought in Will Corsey and his bunch.

It was about that time a couple of homesteaders were trampled to death by stampedes in two separate incidents. Tom McKay egged one settler into a fight at the saloon. Of course, the settler was no match for McKay. McKay gunned him down right there in the saloon. Witness said, "Well, the sodbuster did go for his gun first," or others said they didn't see it happen. Another homesteader just disappeared.

Corsey and his bunch came upon the back steps that led up to Lester Hoch's office. Corsey told McKay, Enos and Kinsel to wait there while he and McGlass went up to talk with Hoch. Of course, Enos started to whine. Corsey turned and started upstairs and began to mumble to McGlass, "I going to kill that sum-bitch, I swear I'm gonna kill him."

Corsey and McGlass reached the top of the stairs; Corsey twisted the doorknob and walked in.

Lester Hoch was setting behind his desk and jumped like he was shot. "JESUS CHRIST," Hoch yelled. "What the hell, don't you ever knock?" he griped. "And what the hell are you doing coming in here, what if someone saw you?"

Corsey strutted over to Hoch's desk and said," Hoch, it's been a week and a half since we made the last hit and you haven't paid up yet. I want my money, NOW," he scowled.

"Our understanding was that you'd get paid when the settlers sell out to me. Spoonhour's wife has not sold yet," Hoch said nervously. "With her man dead, she can't hold out too much longer," he added.

Corsey leaned over the desk and got in Hoch's face. Lester could smell the cheap whiskey on the big man's breath. "You know, I DON'T GIVE A DAMN what our understanding was. All I give a damn about is NOW, and NOW is when I want my money," Corsey bellowed.

Lester was getting nervous; he pulled a handkerchief from his breast pocket and began mopping his brow.

"Okay, okay. I'll pay you now, but you must not come up here anymore," Lester said. "From now on, we need to meet at our designated place," he added.

"We cannot be seen together or this operation will blow up in our face," Lester stated flatly

"Fine, just pay up and add an extra hundred for taking so long," growled Corsey.

"An extra hundred?" Hoch said.

"That's right, any problem with that," Corsey asked.

"NO, NO. That will be okay. It'll be worth it," Hoch said nervously. Lester went into the next room, got the money from his safe and returned. Lester was coming to the realization that it may have been a mistake in hiring this bunch. "Here, now try not to be seen leaving, *please*," Hoch said while handing Corsey the money.

Corsey took the money and quickly counted it and asked, "Got any other sodbuster that needs to be removed?"

"Not now," Lester said. "Listen, Will, we need for this last deal you did to die down first. I heard the federal marshal out of Wichita is starting to nose around, and we don't need any of that right now," Lester said.

Corsey smiled and said, "I'll take care of that marshal just like the others. Just say the word ... same price.

"NO, NO. We don't need that kind of trouble for sure. I'll be in touch," Hoch said. Lester was getting more nervous. He wanted these guys out of there. What if Tray Alexander, the bank president, came in while Corsey and McGlass were here? Hoch shuddered at the thought.

"I'll send my messenger when we need to make another move," Hoch said, "until then stay low."

Corsey turned to leave, then stopped, looked back and said, "Don't be so nervous, Hoch. With Spoonhour out of the way, the rest of those sodbusters will fold." With that Corsey and McGlass left.

Chapter 3

A WEEK AND a half had passed since Jake was shot. Jenny hadn't slept much during that time. She and Julio Sanchez had taken turns at watch and with all the chores to do there was little time for sleep.

Julio was out checking the cattle, which hadn't been checked for a week. There wasn't time, with just the two of them, to look after the place like they should. The morning after Julio sent the word out for VanPelt, the two ranch hands Jake had hired a couple of months before came to Jenny. They gave their apologies and said how sorry they were about what had happened to Jake, but they were cowhands, not gunmen. Both said they had families over in Arkansas they had to think about. They wished Jenny luck and rode off.

Jenny was thinking of all that had happened the last 10 days as she dumped the water basin off the front porch. Jenny turned to go inside when she heard a wren call and it sounded close. As she turned back to see it, she felt a faint breeze move behind her. As Jenny turned to go back into the house, terror moved up her spin.

There, standing before her, was an Indian dressed from head to toe in buckskins.

Jenny screamed and dropped the basin as she brought her hands up to her mouth. Jenny threw her arms around the man's neck and began to sob.

"You made it, I knew you would come," she said over and over, "I knew you would come!"

The man in the buckskins wasn't an Indian. It was Camron VanPelt, a life-long friend of Jake and Jenny Spoonhour. Jake once described VanPelt as "smoke." He said VanPelt would be there one second and then he would be gone.

Camron VanPelt had lived with the Chippewa Indians up north, around eastern Minnesota and southern Michigan, for a number of years. During that period of time VanPelt became an Indian, you might say. His skin was burnt dark by the blazing sun and he learned the Indian ways well and even began to think the way the Chippewa think.

VanPelt moved like an Indian, with quickness and cunning, always without a sound when hunting. Camron could move in and be standing next to a deer in an instant and cut its throat before the deer knew what happened.

VanPelt was a tall man, six one or two, about the same height as Jake, but very lean. His weight was somewhere around 180 to 185 pounds and he was extremely strong for that weight. With a handgun or a knife, there was none faster.

VanPelt had a scar below his right ear, a token from a Sioux Indian who was counting coup one day. Counting coup, as the Indians called it, was nothing more than getting close enough to an enemy to touch him with a knife or lance and then making off without being touched or harmed. To an Indian, this accomplishment was a bigger deal then taking a scalp. The Sioux's count ended that day; he became VanPelt's first kill with a knife.

"Cam, please come in, I've forgotten my manners. Come in." Jake and Jenny were the only ones who could get by with calling him Cam. They turned and started inside.

"Did Jake?" Cam was asking about his close friend when Jenny put a figure to her lips. "Shhhhh, please come this way," she whispered. She took Cam's hand and led him through the house to a back room.

Jenny very gently opened the door to a bedroom and took Cam inside. Lying on the bed, his chest wrapped with clean white bandages was Jake Spoonhour.

VanPelt walked over beside the bed and looked down at his friend. Cam could tell Jake was breathing fairly easy and seemed to be resting okay.

Cam looked up at Jenny. She could tell by the expression on his face that someone was going to pay.

Saying nothing, Jenny motioned with her head to the door. When they were both back at the kitchen table, Jenny poured Cam some hot coffee.

"You always did make the best coffee around," Cam said.

"And you always had the biggest line of bull," Jenny laughed. She felt herself starting to relax, just because he was here.

"What's the story?" Cam asked. He had never been one to beat around the bush.

"What all do you know?" asked Jenny.

"All I know is what Julio put out on the pipeline from the badlands up in the Panhandle," Cam answered. Rumor was, Jake had been shot and I was to come pronto."

Jenny poured herself a cup and sat down at the table with Cam. "Julio told me the pipeline out of the badlands would be the quickest way to get word to you," Jenny stated. "He said most of the people who traveled through there were good people and that just a few bad ones gave the panhandle its name." She continued, "The really bad ones hung out at a place called the Hole-in-the-Wall."

Jenny briefly related the story of what had happened, and how a lot of the settlers had been leaving for one reason or another. She also explained about how some of the settlers had been killed in so-called accidents recently.

Camron stood up and started to move around the kitchen; he never could sit for very long.

"Who's buying up all the land?" Cam asked. "Is it one person or different people buying it up?"

"No one knows for sure. Most of the land is being bought in the names of different companies," she continued. "A lawyer out of Covington handles the transactions. Covington is a town about ten miles north of Marshall."

"What do you know about a man named Corsey, William Corsey?" Cam asked.

"Nothing, I don't think I've ever heard that name. Why?" Jenny asked?

"Don't know for sure. I arrived here a couple of days ago and saw the fresh-dug grave up on the hill. Figured Jake was gone so I went into town to see what I could learn," Cam said as he sat back down and continued telling Jenny how he thought he could find out who might have killed Jake by putting on his drunken Indian act. He explained how he would sit around town, mostly around the saloons and just listen. That's where he heard that Jake was dead.

Jenny told him, "That was Julio's idea; he thought if whoever shot Jake believed he had done the job, it might make it safer for us until you got here. Doc Sherman is the only other person besides Julio and I who knows Jake is still alive. Not even the two hired hands that stayed around a couple of days after the shooting know he survived.

That was also Julio's idea, along with the fake grave," Jenny finished.

Cam said, "Julio is a smart man, you and Jake are lucky to have him. What about this Doc Sherman?"

"Doc Sherman is a good man and he hates what's going on here. I'd trust him with my life," she explained.

"You asked if I knew a William something," Jenny asked.

"Corsey, I don't know," Cam said, thinking. "I saw him in town and was just wondering. Corsey is a killer for hire, and I was thinking he might be our problem, but maybe not," he added.

Cam stood again and walked toward the door. His hat was hanging on a peg by the door where he had placed it when he came in. Cam retrieved his hat, turned and spoke, "Sun's down. I'm going to set up camp in that grove of trees east of the house. I'll have a good view of the place from that ridge, so you get some rest tonight."

Jenny walked over to Cam. "How can we thank you for helping us?"

Cam looked down at her, smiled and said," You don't worry about that. Just take good care of my friend in there. There's not enough of his kind around as it is; we don't what to lose him."

VanPelt stepped through the door and was gone. Jenny was thinking, what a good friend to have.

Chapter 4

V ANPELT SET UP his dry camp that night back in the trees, just as he told Jenny he would and stood watch all night. About 2:00 that morning, Cam began to get a very faint smell of smoke in the air. He stood up and looked around. To the southwest he could see a slight glow. The glow of light looked to be about four to five miles away. Someone was having a bad night, Cam thought to himself.

At daybreak, VanPelt saddled the Appaloosa and headed north. He had passed through the little town of Douglas when coming to Marshall. Cam had stopped at the small general store in Douglas for supplies and while there caught a glimpse of an old friend from many years ago. Not knowing the circumstances surrounding the shooting of Jake Spoonhour at the time, VanPelt thought it best not to make contact with this friend from the past, at least not until Cam knew a little more about what was going on. The old friend's name was Elmer Beals, or Skeeter as the old gang used to call him back home.

Skeeter had spent his growing-up days with Jake and Cam back in Cosby, Tennessee. After surveying the situation, VanPelt had decided he was going to need someone to watch the ranch so he could move about and try to figure out who was responsible for shooting Jake. Skeeter would be perfect for the job. Cam had run into Skeeter at different times through the years since their childhood, and Skeeter hadn't changed a bit. He was still honest as the day is long, just as he was as a boy.

While growing up, Skeeter was the smallest of the three and sometimes needed Jake and Cam to help him out of problems he would get himself into from time to time. Skeeter was always quick-thinking and also quick with his mouth. This got him in trouble with some of the older boys around Cosby. When things got to the point where Skeeter couldn't talk his way out of a problem, Jake and Cam would always step in and bend a few heads. Cam would tell Jake after each time they rescued Skeeter, we should let him get beat to a pulp and maybe he would learn to keep his mouth shut. Jake would always agree, but when time came they were always there to bail Skeeter out.

VanPelt was riding along, staying to the low land as best he could, trying to keep his silhouette from the horizon as much as possible, thinking about the old days and reminiscing when he came upon a riderless horse. The horse was saddled and was standing ground-tied. Cam moved in with caution. As he got closer to the horse, he could see it was a bay and looked to have been ridden hard.

VanPelt stepped down from his horse. He was still about 25 yards away from the other horse, when he noticed some drops of blood on the ground. Cam bent down to get a closer look at the blood when a shot rang out.

VanPelt dropped like a rock, rolled twice and leaped behind a boulder. Another shot sounded, and a bullet ricocheted off the rock he was behind. Cam looked around to see if there might be a way to move from behind the boulder and try to work his way to the other side of whoever was taking target practice at him.

Cam was in a gully, washed out by many years of rainstorms and flash floods. The walls of the gully were 10 to 12 feet high with rough rock and dirt sloping down to the floor. The floor of the gully was about 50 yards across with bushes, clumps of grass and large rocks or boulders scattered all around.

The sun was at Cam's back, so his assailant had to be looking into it. That would be of some help, Cam was thinking as he looked around.

About five yards over VanPelt's shoulder were a few bushes, and behind the bushes was dry creek bed not more than 4 or 5 inches deep. That will have to do, Cam thought.

Cam flattened out and started moving towards the shallow creek bed. He would have cover from the boulder most of the way to the dry creek bed. The last couple of yards might be a different story. Cam's buckskins and leather hat were a reddish brown which were very close to the color of the ground.

Cam made it to the edge of the creek and slid off into it. The shallow dry creek bed angled off to the northwest, and that's the way VanPelt started crawling. The shooter was to his right and the best Cam could figure, about 12 feet above the floor of the gully. There were a number of large rocks at the edge of gully, and that's where Cam thought the gunman was.

Cam continued to crawl along the creek bed. After about 25 yards he came to where the creek had split off to the west, and took a left turn. Soon he was behind an outcropping of rocks and dirt. He could stand now without being seen. Cam took off in a sprint to the west. This portion of the gully was much narrower than the other and offered good cover.

After a few yards the gully turned back to the north and fed back into the main washout. Cam was a good 50 yards farther up the dry creek bed, and by staying low he was able to cross over and get behind the shooter.

Another shot rang out from the gunman, and Cam smiled to himself and thought the guy is getting nervous because he hadn't seen any movement since his prey had leaped behind that rock. He's starting to wonder if one of his bullets had found its mark and was now trying to decide whether he should move out or wait to make sure both of his targets were dead.

If that's what the gunman was thinking, he thought too long. By this time VanPelt was standing directly behind the man and about 20 feet away. Cam said nothing and made no sound.

The man must have got a feeling something or someone was watching him. He slowly turned his head to the left and looked over his shoulder. He caught a glimpse of VanPelt out of the corner of his eye and his face went white.

"YOU SON-OF-A," he yelled, while turning. His rifle got about halfway around when VanPelt's knife buried up to the hilt into the gunman's chest, just above his left breast pocket. His rifle went off into the ground as he fell.

VanPelt always wore his knife and its sheath on his back to the right side of his neck. When Cam reached for his knife, his arm was already in a throwing position.

Cam walked to where the man was slumped over. He reached down and pulled the eight-inch blade out of the man's chest. When the knife was out, blood started to pour out in a steady stream. It was obvious the man took a direct hit in the heart. Cam wiped the blood from his knife blade on the man's shoulder and placed it back in the sheath.

VanPelt pushed the dead man over on his back so he could get a look at his face. Cam didn't recognize the man, so he bent down and went through his pockets to try to find some identification. He found nothing with a name on it, but he did find about twenty dollars in cash and a cheap watch.

VanPelt stood and looked around for the dead man's horse and spotted it tied under a couple of trees about 70 yards to the north and away from the edge of the gully. Cam retrieved the horse and took a mental note of the horse's hoof prints.

Cam loaded the body across the saddle and tied it on. He took the rifle boot from the saddle and put the dead man's rifle in it. He also took the man's gun belt and colt revolver.

After VanPelt had the body situated on the horse, he tied the reins to the saddle horn and slapped the horse on the rump in the hopes he would take his owner back to where he came from.

Cam started down the slop to check out the riderless horse. As he came up to the bay horse, Cam saw another man lying face down under a bush about 20 yards north of the horse. When VanPelt got to the man, he could see a bad wound on the upper right portion of the man's back. It was obvious the man had lost a lot of blood.

Cam very gently turned the man over and checked his pulse. He had a pulse, but it was very faint. Cam put the man's hat under his head, trying to make him a little more comfortable.

Cam could smell wood smoke on the man's clothes and also noticed some charcoal smudges on him.

VanPelt went to his own horse and retrieved his water bag and then went back to the man. He poured some water onto his bandana and squeezed a few drops of water into the man's mouth, then wiped his face.

The man started to breathe very heavy, like it was a real effort. He coughed a couple of times and moved his lips as if to speak.

"Who did this to you?" Cam asked the man. Cam moved his ear down close to the man's mouth and strained to hear.

The man said, "They burnt my place," he coughed again, "burnt my place," he repeated. With that the man died.

Cam checked his pockets, and all he found was an envelope addressed to a Howard Reed, Marshall, Oklahoma Territory. The return address was the Territory Land Company, Covington, Oklahoma Territory. The letter inside was an offer to buy Mr. Reed's homestead. The letter was postmarked about a month ago.

VanPelt assumed the man to be Howard Reed since that was the name on the letter but there still were a number of unanswered questions. Like who was the shooter? How far had Mr. Reed come before he went down? From the looks of the wound, it was apparent Reed was shot somewhere else, rode to this spot and could go no farther. Plus, if that was the case, what was the shooter doing there if Reed was shot somewhere else?

Cam was mulling all this over in his mind as he loaded Reed over the saddle on the bay. Cam also noticed Mr. Reed was unarmed. He had no weapon at all. So, Reed was unarmed, shot in the back and about 15 miles from home.

Cam gathered up his horse and continued on his way to Douglas. He would take Howard Reed into town for a proper burial.

VanPelt continued thinking about what had happened as he rode. Reed was shot in the back; maybe he was trying to get away or running from someone, possibly the shooter. Reed had said they burned his place, and he had a strong smell of wood smoke.

Cam suddenly pulled up and stopped. "That's it," he said to himself. The glow and the faint smell of wood smoke last night. That was probably Reed's place and they, whoever they are, burned him out last night. Reed may have been trying to get away and was shot in the back as he rode off. The shooter must have followed Reed to finish the job and then I came along. Cam considered this as he continued on.

Chapter 5

VANPELT RODE INTO Douglas about noon leading the bay with Mr. Reed draped over the saddle. He stepped down from his horse in front of the sheriff's office. The sheriff was standing in the doorway.

Your partner don't look very comfortable ridin' like that," the sheriff said.

"He doesn't care much right now," Cam answered back with a slight smile as he tied both horses to the hitching post.

The sheriff stepped aside to let Cam into the office. The sheriff introduced himself: "I'm Sheriff Darrah; Forest Darrah," he offered his hand to VanPelt.

"VanPelt, Camron VanPelt," Cam said and shook the sheriff's hand.

VanPelt told Sheriff Darrah the story of how he came upon Howard Reed and gave the sheriff the envelope he had found in Reed's pocket. Cam also filled Darrah in on what was going on around Marshall and how his friend had been shot and all the shady activity going on over there. Cam left out the fact that his friend, Jake Spoonhour, had survived the shot.

"Where's the body of the shooter, the guy that you think shot Reed?" Darrah asked.

"I tied the body to his horse and gave him his head. I'm thinking his horse might go back to his barn or to where he is fed regular," Cam said. "On my way back I'll try to pick up his tracks and see where they lead."

"That's a good idea and I don't have to deal with his burial. Let me know if you turn up anything on that hombre," Darrah added.

"Here's the twenty dollars I took off the shooter. That should take care of burying Mr. Reed," Cam said, handing Sheriff Darrah the money. "Also, I have the shooter's guns that I'll leave with you."

VanPelt went out and retrieved the guns and gave them to the sheriff. A small group of townspeople had gathered around the dead man and were wondering what was going on. The sheriff followed

VanPelt outside and was standing on the boardwalk.

"All you folks move along. Nothin' here for you to worry about," the sheriff said.

VanPelt had untied his horse and was leading him across the dusty street to a watering trough when he saw Skeeter Beals walking up the boardwalk toward him.

"Someone back in the saloon said some half-Indian-lookin' hombre brought in a dead body stretched across a saddle and I thought to myself, dead body — half-Indian-lookin', VanPelt must be in town."

"How ya doin'? You old canoe bottom," Skeeter said with a laugh.

"Good, my friend, and how are you?" Cam answered with a big smile.

Skeeter came back with," I couldn't be better myself. What brings you to these parts? Are you just delivering bodies?"

"I'm needin' some help," Cam said.

"No problem," Skeeter snapped." I'll get my horse," he said as he turned to go to the livery stable.

"Wait, don't you want to know what you're getting yourself into?" Cam asked.

"Don't matter. If you need help, I'm there. You can tell me the details on the way," Skeeter said flatly and continued on to get his horse.

VanPelt and Skeeter rode out to the gully where Cam had his run-in with the shooter earlier that day. Cam had filled Skeeter in on what was going on as they rode along. Skeeter agreed with Cam's theory about Mr. Reed and how he got to where VanPelt had found him.

They picked up the tracks of the shooter's horse in no time and began to follow them. After about an hour it looked like the horse was heading back to Marshall or at least in that direction.

The horse tracks took VanPelt and Beals within about a mile of Jake and Jenny's place. The two men turned off the horse trail they had been following and headed for the ranch.

As they rode up to the house, Julio came out of the barn with his rifle pointed at the two riders. Jenny came running out of the house yelling to Julio to put down his rifle and that it was okay.

"These men are our friends. They are here to help us." Jenny yelled. "Please come in, Skeeter, It's been forever since we've see you," she whispered as she gave him a hug.

VanPelt stepped down from his horse and extended his hand to Julio. "Jenny tells me she and Jake couldn't have made it without you," Cam said. "My name is Camron VanPelt; I've been a friend of Jake and Jenny's for a long time. This here's Skeeter Beals — we all kind of grew up together," introducing Beals.

"I've heard a lot about you, Señor." Señora Jenny speaks very well of you. Welcome, Señor," Julio said with a smile.

"You gentlemen must come in. Jake is awake and will want to see ya both," Jenny said. "He is still very weak but gettin' stronger every day. After you men talk, I'll have supper ready. Julio, you'll eat with us, too?"

Julio didn't reply; he just put on an ear-to-ear grin.

Jenny led Cam and Skeeter to the back room and eased the door open. "You have company," she said as she stepped aside.

Jake looked like hell and Cam told him as much. Skeeter, never one to be at a loss for words, agreed with Cam and said, "You look like you fell out of an ugly tree and hit every branch on the way down."

Jake tried to laugh, but it hurt too much. He began to cough, which prompted Jenny to scold their two guests. "If you three," she included Jake, "don't behave, there'll be no supper for any of ya!"

"Okay, okay," Cam said, "this would be the only time Skeeter and I can get away with teasing him. If he was up and about, he'd kick our butts."

"It's good to see you guys," Jake said with a raspy whisper, just barely loud enough to hear. " 'Course, it's good to be able to see anything."

Cam and Skeeter moved in closer to Jake's bedside. "Ya got any ideas about who might have done this?" Cam asked.

"No," Jake said and started to cough. Jenny moved in. "That's enough for now, Jake. You need to get some rest."

Jake held his hand up. "Jenny, I'm okay, give me just a second. There is something our friends need to know." Jake paused. "I don't know who did the shooting, but I saw Pat McGlass in town about, oh, I don't know," he paused again. "I've lost track of time, but I think it was two or three days before this happened. Where McGlass crawls," he continued, "Will Corsey ain't too far behind."

"Save your strength," Cam touched Jake's shoulder. "I was in town yesterday and saw the whole bunch. There was McGlass and

Corsey all right with Tom McKay, Jim Enos and Dave Kinsel. What we need to figure out is who is payin' that bunch. Ya know," he went on, "they wouldn't be stayin' around unless there was easy money to be made."

"Show's over, rest time," Jenny said as she started pushing Skeeter toward the door.

"She's right, Jake," Cam said. "We'll check ya later. I'm going to do a little snoopin' around in town tonight. Skeeter is going to watch the place along with his old Sharps 50 caliber to talk to tonight while I'm in town, so you two get some sleep."

VanPelt backed out of Jake's room and eased the door closed. Cam looked at Skeeter and could read his face like a book. He knew Skeeter was feeling the same way he felt. "Skeeter, we're going to get the person or people responsible for that," Cam said with a motion to Jake's room, "and that is a promise."

Skeeter nodded his head and said, "You got that right, old pard."

"Okay, boys," Jenny said, handing each a cup of hot coffee, "You two sit and relax. I'll have some supper ready in no time." With that, she was off to the kitchen.

Cam and Skeeter took a chair and began shootin' the bull and going over the few facts they had. Soon Jenny had supper on the table and called Julio to join them.

They had a very pleasant meal and enjoyed telling Julio old stories on each other. Finally the men had eaten their fill and it was time Cam started for town. Skeeter volunteered to do the dishes and wouldn't have it any other way.

Jenny and Skeeter walked Cam out on the front porch.

VanPelt turned to face Jenny and said, "As we were coming in, I showed Skeeter the grove of trees up on the ridge where he and I will keep watch. At least one of us will be there every night for a while. I'm heading into town tonight to see what I can hear."

"Skeeter, I'll be back about midnight and give you a whistle before I come into camp," Cam said as he swung into his saddle.

Jenny grabbed Skeeter by the arm and led him inside the house, just a talkin' as fast as she could about old times.

Chapter 6

VANPELT HEADED BACK and picked up the tracks he and Skeeter had been following. The trail did lead into Marshall as VanPelt thought, so he pulled up short of the town and skirted around the edge. He held up under some trees and waited until sundown.

When the sun was down, Cam tied his horse well back in the clump of trees and started walking toward the backside of a row of buildings.

There wasn't much moonlight that night, and the moon was showing a faint ring around it. A ring around the moon was a pretty good sign rain was coming within 48 hours.

The best place to hear gossip in these small towns was the barbershop. But to get closer to the truth, the editor of the local newspaper was usually the place.

VanPelt walked to the back of the buildings and kept low while moving along. As he went, he peered through the windows looking for the paper office. He knew it was on this side of the street, but which building he wasn't sure.

VanPelt suddenly heard men coming through the space between two buildings. He crouched behind a rain barrel as they came closer.

"All I'm sayin' is, ten bucks ain't much for burnin' a place," one of the men was complaining.

"Whose place?" VanPelt said as he stood.

The two men had already passed the rain barrel that VanPelt had ducked behind. They nearly jumped out of their skin when VanPelt spoke. One of the men was carrying a bottle of whiskey. He cursed and dropped his bottle at the same time.

The other man turned and started to draw his handgun. VanPelt was ready with his hand behind his neck. Cam drew his knife and hit the man on the right side of his head with the butt of the knife. The man dropped to the ground in a heap. The other man stood wide-eyed with his hands out in front of him with the palms up.

"Don't cut me, Injun; I didn't do nothin' to you," the man begged.

"Whose place did you burn?" VanPelt asked again.

"Don't know what you're talkin' about," the man answered. The alcohol was helping him get a little courage back.

"Besides, I don't havta tell no damned Injun nothin'," he said as he raised his chin a little. As his chin went up, VanPelt flashed the point of his knife under the man's chin. The man was on his toes now and was trying to keep his balance so he wouldn't come down on the knife. "Please don't," is all the man got out before VanPelt interrupted, "Who shot Jake Spoonhour?" Cam lowered the knife just enough to let the man speak.

"I had nothin' to do with that. No, sir, nothin' to do with that. I don't know who did it. We're cowhands, not gunmen," he whimpered.

"Who paid ya to burn someone's place," Cam asked, pushing the knife up a little.

"I don't know. I don't know," the man squealed. "We got our orders and our pay by messenger. We never saw or talked to nobody," he said breathlessly.

"Who was the messenger?" VanPelt wanted to know.

"Some half-wit kid. I didn't know him," he said.

The other man moaned and started to move a little.

"Get your friend and get out of town. If I see either one of you again, I'll cut your gizzards out," VanPelt promised. "Now get."

The cowhand grabbed his buddy and cleared out as fast as he could.

VanPelt continued down the backside of the buildings and finally came upon the newspaper office. He could see only one man in the printing area bent over a printing press.

Cam tried the door. It was unlocked. He stepped inside and pulled the window shade down behind him.

"Jimmy, bring me that new bottle of ink over there," the man said, without looking up.

VanPelt looked around and saw a bottle of printer's ink on a shelf by the door. He picked it up and delivered it to the man. The man reached out, took the bottle and still didn't look up. The man continued to work for a second longer, and then he stopped. He stood up right and turned slightly. He was looking directly at VanPelt's chest. His head continued upward until he was looking into Cam's face.

"You're not Jimmy," the gentleman gulped and started to shake.

"You're going to drop that bottle of ink if ya don't watch it," Cam said with a half-smile.

The little man grabbed the bottle with both hands and set it down.

"What do you want?" the little man said nervously.

"My name is Camron VanPelt, and your name is?" Cam extended his hand as he spoke.

"Stephen Snell," he answered very cautiously while pushing his eyeglasses back up his nose.

VanPelt briefly explained why he was there and also told Mr. Snell about Howard Reed and the shooter. Cam asked Snell if he saw the horse with the man strapped over the saddle come into town.

Snell related to VanPelt how much excitement that had caused. Snell told Cam that the horse came trotting down Main Street and pulled up right in front of the livery stable. It seems the man worked for one of the land companies that were buying up homesteads around the county. He continued to say that a number of people gathered around the body, and some were wondering how someone got close enough to Talbott to stick a knife into him. "That was his name, Al Talbott. They were saying Talbott was pretty good with a rifle."

"What have you heard about the shooting of Jake Spoonhour?" Cam asked.

"Hadn't been much talk about Jake other than how everyone hated to hear about him getting killed, especially me. I considered Jake a friend," Snell answered.

VanPelt told Snell about his friendship with Jake and Jenny and how he was here to find out who shot Jake. Cam also told Snell to keep it to himself that he was around, at least for awhile.

"You can count on me, Mr. VanPelt. Any friend of the Spoonhours must be all right, and I will keep an ear open for any information that might be of help," Snell assured Cam.

"Thanks," Cam said as he moved to the back door. He checked outside before opening the door and was gone.

VanPelt went back to the alleyway that ran between two buildings and moved with care to the front boardwalk. He checked up and down the street in both directions. There looked to be normal movement going on, mostly in and out of the saloon. The sounds of laughter and an old, not-played-too-well piano filtered down the street. A lamplighter was tending to his job on the far side of the street.

VanPelt crossed to the other side of the street and leaned up against the wall to the left of the batwing doors of the Shotgun Saloon.

A drunk staggered out of the saloon and stumbled down the steps before falling head first into the dusty street. A few minutes later another man came out looking one way, then the other. He stopped in the middle of boardwalk, "John. John," he spoke a little louder. "JOHN," he was yelling now. The first man, lying in the street, moaned and turned over. "John, there ya are, buddy. I thought you were gonna dance with that looker in there," the second man said.

John leaned up on one arm and started to mumble, "Dan. Dan. Dan, is that you? Dan, help me up. Dan, I thought I WAS dancin' with some gal, only thing was, her breath smelled like dust," he slobbered.

Dan went down the steps and with much effort helped his good buddy get up, and the two friends staggered back inside. Cam just smiled and shook his head.

VanPelt was beginning to think this might have been a worthless trip when he heard riders coming down the street. He eased farther back into the shadows and waited.

As the riders pulled up in front of the saloon, one of them was moaning and said, "You got to get me a doc, my hand is blown apart."

"Shut the hell up. I need a drink. 'Sides, the doc is probably in the saloon anyhow," growled one of the other men.

There were three of them, and as they stepped up on the boardwalk and moved into the light that shone through the saloon door, VanPelt could make out their features. The big one was unmistakable. It was Tom McKay. The one who was moaning and groaning about his hand was that low-life Dave Kinsel. The third man was Jim Enos.

VanPelt was wondering where they had been and what had happened to Kinsel's hand. Whatever they had been up to, they must not have fared too well.

After the three had gone inside, VanPelt headed back across the street and retraced his steps to his horse. He decided he would come back tomorrow and have a visit with Doc Sherman.

VanPelt mounted and made his way through the trees until he was a good distance from town and was sure no one had followed him. He arrived back to where Skeeter was dry-camped above the ranch. It was about 1 a.m. when Cam gave a wren whistle to let Skeeter know he was coming in. Skeeter answered Cam's signal with one of his own to give VanPelt the all-clear. Cam moved in and was standing about 10 feet behind Skeeter.

"Everything good," Cam spoke quietly.

Skeeter jumped like he was shot. "You ding bust it ... sorry ... dog's hind leg. Your whistle came from over that way."

Cam was grinning as he came on into camp. "The Chippewa showed me that little trick of throwin' your whistle so it sounds like it's comin' from another direction. All quiet here?" he asked.

"It is now, but I had me some fun earlier with some fire totin' hombres," Skeeter said.

Skeeter proceeded to relay the details of what had taken place earlier in the evening. Beals began with how his horse's nervousness had alerted him to riders approaching the ranch. The riders had reined up in the stream that ran about 300 yards in front of the ranch house. Skeeter said he could barely make out the riders in the dim moonlight that reflected off the stream. There were three of them, and as they sat in the middle of the stream water, one of the men struck a match and lit a torch. He handed the torch to one of the other men and proceeded to light another.

"Well," Skeeter continued, "that's when I decided to change their way of thinkin' into another direction."

Skeeter went on to say that even though the riders were a good 200 yards away, the torches helped him see the outline of all three men. Skeeter picked out the man who had taken the first torch and leveled a bead about a foot down and to the left of the flame.

"I figured that would put my slug right square with his body." Skeeter raised his shoulders and dropped them. "But I guess his horse shifted weight and moved back a little at the same time I squeezed off the Sharps, because the shot knocked the torch out of his hand and into the water. You know I don't miss my targets that bad," frowned Skeeter.

"Anyhow, the guy holding the other torch dropped his in the water, too, and they all turned tail and lit a shuck out of there," Skeeter explained, smiling.

"You're a better shot than you think," Cam offered and proceeded to tell Skeeter where he had been and about seeing McKay, Enos and Kinsel.

"So your slug found a mark, just not the mark you were aiming at. Kinsel will never have much use of his right hand again and that was his gun hand," Cam said, thinking about it. "The other good thing is, you saved Jake and Jenny from being burned out," he finished with a slap on Skeeter's back. "Good job."

"You get some rest," Cam said. "I'll take first watch and wake ya in about three hours and we'll trade off. In the morning we'll check on Jake and then maybe ride over and take a look at what is left of Howard Reed's place."

With that, Skeeter went over to where he had rolled out his bed and soon was sound asleep.

Chapter 7

THE NEXT MORNING at daybreak, Skeeter started rustling up some grub; jerked beef and hardtack was about it. He did build a small smokeless fire and put a pot on to boil some coffee. VanPelt came alive with the smell of coffee. He traded his moccasins for a pair of boots from his saddlebag, shook both of them out and stomped his feet into them. One of the first things a man on the trail learns is to shake out anything that was on the ground the night before. Many was the time some night critter, like a scorpion, has tumbled out of a cowhand's gear and not in a very good mood.

"We might be in the saddle a lot today," Cam said while pulling his pant legs down over the boot tops. "Boots will be a bit more comfy in the stirrups."

"There's the difference between you and me," Skeeter deadpanned. "You'll never catch me walkin' enough to warrant ownin' a pair of them moccasins."

"That's not the ONLY difference between us," Cam said, looking away so Skeeter couldn't see his slight grin.

"Son of a …" Skeeter mumbled and spit tobacco juice from his first morning chew.

"What was that? Couldn't hear ya," Cam teased while pouring his cup full of hot coffee.

They both had a chuckle and sat down to eat. After eating, they saddled up and rode down out of the trees toward the ranch house. Jenny was in good spirits, mainly because Jake was on his way to recovery. It would still be a while before Jake could be up and about, much less do any work, but he did look better. Cam and Skeeter being around to watch the place had a lot to do with Jake's peace of mind, and Jenny said as much.

Cam, along with Skeeter, filled in the detail and relayed to both Jake and Jenny about last night's goings-on and assured them there was no reason for concern. Cam laid out his plan of, with the help of Skeeter and Julio, keeping a close eye on things and how everything should be covered. After a quick cup of coffee, both Cam and Skeeter mounted up and headed southwest toward the Reed place.

It took the better part of two hours for the two to cover the five miles to the Reed homestead. Still not wanting to attract any attention, Cam and Skeeter traveled in the trees or stayed to the low ground as much as possible.

When they neared the location where the house and barn once stood, Cam motioned to Skeeter to swing around and approach from a different direction. Cam waited a few minutes to give Skeeter time to move around to the back of the place before he started forward.

Both men urged their horses in slowly. Beals gave the all-clear signal from his view and Cam gave it back. They rode on in and stepped down from their horses, taking care not to disturb any tracks that might help tell the story of what happened here.

VanPelt squatted near the barn to take a closer look at a number of tracks still visible in the dirt. Cam pointed to a faint hoof mark in the dust as he spoke, "Looks like our shooter was here all right. Guess we had it figured pretty close. Over there," he pointed to another track, "Is where the shooter took out kinda' fast-like, probably spotted Howard Reed trying to get away and chased after him."

"I don't see any tracks that match our last night visitors to the ranch. McKay's horse leaves a real deep print 'cause of all the weight he's a-carrying," Skeeter observed.

VanPelt agreed as he stood, "I make it to be four, maybe five riders. That how you see it?"

Beals nodded as he looked about, "Not much left of the barn or the house. Shame, this here was a nice place."

VanPelt and Beals looked around the burned-out remains for about a half-hour, moving and turning over things. Looking for anything that might give a clue to who may have been responsible for starting the fire. They found nothing of any help.

"Let's head on into town; I want to have a talk with Doc Sherman," VanPelt said as he stepped into his saddle "Maybe the Doc has heard something."

VanPelt and Beals started toward town, but not before they circled the outer perimeter of the homestead to observe and take mental note of all the different tracks they could find.

VanPelt and Beals skirted the outer edge of Marshall and rode into town from the south. Cam always circled around so as not to enter from the same direction he was actually coming from.

"I'm a little parched," Skeeter said while rubbing his throat. "What ya say to wettin' our whistles just a mite?"

"That sounds pretty good," Cam answered with a motion. "Doc's office is the building this side of the Shotgun Saloon, over there to your right."

Both men stepped down from their mounts and loosely tied the reins to the hitching post in front of a two-story building with sign painted on the window in large gold lettering that read: "Doctor Lawrence Sherman MD." There was a space, about the width of two wagons sitting side by side, between Doc Sherman's building and the Shotgun Saloon.

Cam and Skeeter walked around the back end of their horses and was about to step up on the boardwalk which ran in front of the saloon, when two rather large town women were coming down from the steps.

"Afternoon, ladies, ain't it a beautiful day?" Skeeter said, while removing his hat he took a deep bow.

The two ladies lifted their noses in disgust and looked the other way, while quickening their step in an effort to get away a little faster.

"Skeeter," Cam said, "you will never change."

"What'd I do? You know that made the day for those two fine ladies," Skeeter retorted with a smile. "You know, as well as I do, they're just a-goin' on to each other 'bout that hansome young man that spoke to them."

Cam just shook his head as he pushed one side of the batwing doors open and moved inside the saloon.

The saloon looked to be quiet with not many customers. The big clock on the wall chimed, telling all concerned it was 3:30. Skeeter followed Cam to the far end of the bar on right side of the room.

The Shotgun Saloon was like most saloons. There were a number of round tables with chairs spread out on both sides of the door with a long bar along the back wall of the room. There was a space for the bartender to move back and forth, and a huge mirror hung on the very back wall with glasses and bottles of whiskey lined up on the back bar beneath the mirror. A sign to the right side of the mirror laid down the ground rules: "No shooting, cutting, fighting or loud cussing allowed and absolutely no spitting on the floor."

At the other end of the bar were two typical cowhands with one of the workin' ladies standing between them acting as if she enjoyed being there. A card game was going on at a table, not too far from the two cowhands, with four men and another workin' lady watching the game. On the same side of the room as Cam and Skeeter, at a table over close to the front wall, were two Mexican-looking hombres with a bottle sitting between them, enjoying their drinks. VanPelt took all this in with a single glance around the room.

"What'll it be, gents?" Shotgun Simmons asked as he wiped the bar using a white towel with one hand, while cradling the ever-present shotgun in the other arm.

"Beer, cold beer if'n ya got it," Skeeter said.

"It'll be cool; we got a dugout to keep it in. Ice is scarce in these parts, specially this time of year. How 'bout you, mister?" the bartender nodded at Cam.

"Same," Cam replied.

Simmons disappeared through a door just to the right of the back bar and returned a couple of minutes later with the two mugs of beer.

The batwings squeaked and Cam glanced out of the corner of his eye to see Dave Kinsel coming through the doors. Kinsel slowly walked over to the center of the bar, about 15 feet from where Cam and Skeeter were standing. Cam and Skeeter made eye contact with each other but made no expression.

Kinsel looked bad. His face was drawn and very pale. "Whiskey," he said with slurred effort. As he spoke, using his left hand Kinsel pulled his right hand and arm up and gently placed it on the bar. He was wearing a leather glove over the right hand, and a small piece of dirty white bandage cloth could be seen hanging out.

Skeeter, without moving his head, glanced at Cam and gave him a half-ornery smile. Cam's expression never changed.

Shotgun Simmons placed a bottle of gut rot in front of Kinsel and stepped down the bar to where the shot glasses were kept. Simmons put the glass on the bar and slid it to Kinsel.

Without thinking, Kinsel stopped the glass with his gloved right hand. He instantly let out a howl of pain, and his face looked twisted and contorted. "SON OF A BITCH," he bellowed. "I otta kill you!"

"Well, if you didn't want a glass, you should have said so," Simmons said with a quizzical look. "But if'n anyone's goin' die here today, it more'n likely will be you," he said while motioning to his shotgun.

As bad as Kinsel's hand was hurting, he knew he had better drop the subject. Kinsel just grunted, grabbed the bottle with his left hand, found the nearest chair and flopped down, taking a long pull on the bottle.

Cam swallowed the last of his beer, nudged Skeeter and nodded at the door. Skeeter quaffed down his beer and started to follow Cam toward the door. As he neared where Kinsel was sitting, Skeeter just couldn't resist the opportunity. He leaned down and with a low voice spoke to Kinsel, "Ya know, those torches can play hell with a man's hand when they blowup like that." Skeeter continued on to the door and caught up to Cam as he was going out.

Kinsel just sat there and took another long drink from the bottle. Being the dim-wit that he was, it took him a couple of minutes to realize what Skeeter had said to him. He finally putting two and two together, figuring out that to know about the torch, that man must have been the one who had shot his hand.

Anger suddenly distorted all of Kinsel's thinking. He jumped from the chair and headed for the batwings. Once outside, he quickly looked to his left. Nothing, he looked to his right. Cam and Skeeter were just stepping from the dirt alley to the boardwalk on the other side.

Kinsel started for them, his rage building. He pulled his gun with his left hand from his belt where he now carried it due to his right hand being out of commission and started down the steps on the saloon side of the alley.

"I'm goin'," is all he got out. As Kinsel stepped down, the heel of his boot caught on the edge of the first step, causing him to fall.

Cam and Skeeter heard the "I'm goin' " and turned around just in time to see Kinsel falling forward with his gun in his left hand. As Kinsel fell, he loosened his grip of the gun handle, causing it to spin upward as he was going down.

Kinsel must have been trying to break his fall by putting his left hand to the ground, and as he did the butt of the gun hit the ground and went off. The gun muzzle was pointed up, right beneath Kinsel's chin. The bullet entered just below his chin and went out the backside of his head, making a much larger hole as it came out and causing a real mess.

Cam looked at Skeeter with a puzzled expression. Skeeter raised his eyebrows into an arch and dropped them to a frown. "I've been to Kansas City to see the elephant, but I ain't never seen anything like that," Skeeter said, while shaking his head.

"What did you say to him as we were leaving the saloon?" Cam asked.

"Just that he otta use more reliable torches or something to that effect," Skeeter answered.

By now a crowd started to gather, and a big-bellied man with a badge pushed his way between the on lookers. "What's going on here? Who shot this man? Did either one of you two have anything to do with this?" he asked while looking directly at VanPelt and then at Beals?

"No, no, they didn't," a voice came from behind Cam and Skeeter. "That man fell on his own gun, causing it to fire. He shot himself. I saw the whole thing," a man in a black broadcloth suit was saying as he walked past Cam and Skeeter.

"And just who the hell are you?" the sheriff huffed.

"Name's Fossett. Bill Fossett, I'm the U.S. Marshal out of Wichita, Kansas. And you would be Sheriff Pool?" the Marshal asked.

W.D. "Bill" Fossett was a well-known lawman who trailed and fought most of the noted bad men in an area which encompassed parts of Oklahoma and Kansas.

"Yes, sir, Sheriff Larry Pool at your service," Pool answered with a much more humble tone. After a couple of awkward seconds, the Sheriff looked around at the crowd and barked, "Okay, some of you gents standing around here pick this mess up and take him back of the barber shop so's Ed can build him a box. The rest of ya clear outa' here."

The Marshal turned back to face VanPelt and Beals, "That hombre did look as if he had a major dislike for one of you two. Know what that was all about?"

Skeeter glanced at Cam and said, "No, sir, first time we really ever see that feller was back there in the saloon just about ten minutes ago. Must have mistook one of us for someone he hated is all I can figure."

"How 'bout you?" the Marshal nodded at VanPelt.

"Might have seen him round town a couple of times," Cam answered evenly. "Marshal, I was about to pay the Doc here a visit," VanPelt gestured to Doc Sherman's office, "on another matter and I'd be obliged if you would join me. There are some things going on around here that you might otta know about."

"I didn't catch your name," Fossett said as he extended his hand.

"My name's VanPelt; this here is Skeeter Beals," VanPelt answered with a handshake.

Skeeter started down the steps, and looking over his shoulder, he said, "I'm gonna pick up some supplies over at the mercantile, while you two are a-jawin' with the Doc. I'll catch ya later." Skeeter untied the reins to his horse, and after a pause at the edge of the street to let a buckboard go by, led the horse across.

VanPelt turned and with the Marshal following entered Doc Sherman's office.

The inside of the office was typical of most frontier doctors' offices. The front room was small with a single roll-top desk shoved against the wall on the left as you walked in and four wooden chairs lined up on the opposite side of the room for patients to sit in while waiting to see the doc. There was a double-wide door opening with white curtains drawn across it on the back wall. That door, more than likely, led to the doc's examining and operating room. A bell on the door signaled VanPelt and the Marshal's entrance with a tinkle.

Soon a slightly built man with white hair and long bushy side whiskers of the same color pushed between the curtains and walked into the room, wiping his hands with a white towel.

"What can I do for you gents?" he asked, while casting a quizzical eye over the man dressed in buckskins.

"You Doc Sherman?" It was obvious, but to be sure Cam had to ask.

"That's right, and you must be VanPelt?" Doc quizzed back. "I'd know you anywhere after hearin' Jenny go on about ya. Jake and Jenny sure think a lot of you."

"I think a lot of them, too, that's why I'm here," Cam said as he turned to Fossett. "This is Bill Fossett. He's the U.S. Marshal out of Wichita," Cam continued as the two men shook hands.

VanPelt proceeded to tell the Marshal all he knew about the deteriorating situation involving the homesteaders in the area and Doc Sherman filled in with what he knew, which wasn't much.

Chapter 8

Iᴛ ᴛᴏᴏᴋ Sᴋᴇᴇᴛᴇʀ about 15 minutes to stock up on enough supplies, beans, coffee and the like to last Cam and himself for at least a week at their camp site. Skeeter had packed the supplies into two flour sacks and was tying them across the back of his saddle when he felt the barrel of a gun nudging him in the small of his back. A low, raspy voice ordered, "You make the wrong move and I'll put daylight through ya. Now, take up the reins of that there hoss and start walkin' real easy, like nothin's goin' on, and head down the alley toward the back of this here buildin'. And remember, get squirrelly and you're a dead man."

Skeeter turned slowly to his left and started down the alley leading his horse just as he had been told. After a couple of steps, Skeeter sensed the presence of his captor on the right and a little behind him. Skeeter felt a sudden pull at his gun. He automatically stopped and felt an empty holster.

"Keep movin'," the man growled.

"Okay, okay, take it easy. What's this all about?" Skeeter asked cautiously.

"Shut up, you don't ask the questions. Now get in there," said the man as they came to a small shack that was located behind the mercantile but was not connected.

The man yanked the reins from Beals' hand and shoved him toward a door in the front of the shack.

Skeeter turned the doorknob and stepped inside with the man following close behind. It was a one-room shack with one window on the back wall that was the only source of light.

Skeeter could barely make out a looming figure of someone to his right. He scanned the other side of the room. His eyes were becoming more accustomed to the dim light. He could make out an even larger outline of a man hulking in the far-left corner.

"Have a chair, friend," the man to his right spoke as he kicked a wooden chair that slide to the center of the room.

"I been sittin' all day, think I'll just stand," Skeeter said in a very quiet guarded voice as he realized he was probably in trouble.

The man behind Beals brought the barrel of his gun down on the back of Skeeter's head with a thud. A bright light went off in Skeeter's head as he dropped to his knees. He was semi-conscious and his head was throbbing.

"Don't mind if I do have a seat," Beals slurred as he half-staggered and half-crawled toward the chair.

"You're a smart mouth son of a bitch, ain't ya?" the man who had hit Beals said as he stepped to the right side of Beals and kicked him in the ribs.

Beals groaned while falling to his left side and began struggling to breathe. The man who had abducted Skeeter at gunpoint was the same one who was now working him over. The man bent down and started to yell in Beal's face, "What's your name and who's your Indian sidekick?"

Beals caught a glimpse of the man's face as he leaned down into the light coming from the small widow. It was Jim Enos. That meant the other two men in the room were probably McGlass and McKay.

Enos grabbed up Beals and shoved him into the chair and yelled again, "Who's that Indian-lookin' hombre you're ridin' with and why did Kinsel go gunnin' for you two?"

Enos backhanded Beals across the mouth when he didn't answer, splitting his lip open and starting a stream of blood running down his chin.

"Talk, you son a bitch," Enos shouted again. Enos was enjoying this; he was too much of a coward to face a man in a fair fight so he was acting like the big man.

"Hold it," McGlass spoke. Enos backed up out of the way as Pat McGlass pulled over another chair and straddled it in front of Beals.

"Now mister..." McGlass began and paused.

"Beals, Skeeter Beals," Skeeter answered with a bloody slur. Skeeter figured if he was going to die he damn sure wanted his killers to know who he was.

"Mr. Beals," McGlass continued in a soft, almost soothing voice." You're going to die one way or the other. If you tell us what we want to know, you can die quick, or we can drag this thing out for a couple of days. It's really up to you and how you want to play it out. Now, who is the hombre in the buckskin?"

Skeeter's mind was racing fast, but he immediately realized his best chance to live was not to tell them anything. He would try to hold out in the hopes that either they would make a mistake or he would get a chance to make a break for it.

"Oh, that old Indian. I just keep him around to run errands for me," Skeeter coughed.

McGlass dropped his head, "Have it your way." He looked over Beals' right shoulder and nodded, then stood and dragged the chair back out of the way.

A monster of a man was now towering over Beals. It was Tom McKay. McKay put both hands on his knees and looked into Beals' eyes.

"I'm going to kill you with my bare hands and then I'm gonna hunt down your Injun friend and shoot him like the dog that he is," McKay growled.

Skeeter looked right back into McKay's cold gray eyes and spoke very clearly, "He'll put a bullet between your eyes before your gun ever clears leather."

McKay's face instantly turned beet red. His cruel eyes opened wide. Without a word he put his huge right fist into the middle of Skeeter's face. The force of the blow knocked Beals over backward and out of the chair. Beals lay in an unconscious crumpled heap with blood streaming from his mouth and nose.

McKay was still fuming from the thought of someone being faster with a gun than he was. McKay walked over and kicked Beals in the rib cage. The kick broke at least a couple of ribs, but Skeeter was out and didn't feel a thing.

McKay whirled about to face McGlass, his features were twisted with rage as he spoke, "That Injun-lookin' son a bitch is mine. I'll gun him down in the street so's everybody knows I'm the fastest gun around! He's mine."

"He's yours," McGlass said with disgust, and then continued, "You sure fixed that one," he nodded at Beals, "He ain't gonna be answering any of our questions for awhile."

"To hell with him, I need a drink," McKay grunted and headed for the door.

McGlass motioned to Enos and then to Beals, "Tie him up, Jim, and do it right. I don't want him getting away till we get some answers."

McGlass followed McKay out the door as Enos started his usual whining, while grabbing a rope that was hanging on the wall just behind the door. He tied Beals' feet and hands behind his back and cinched both up tight to where his hands were almost touching his feet. Enos double-checked his work, and in an effort to catch up with McGlass and McKay quickly left the shack after securing the door with a rusted padlock. Beals faded in and out of consciousness for the next couple of hours. When he was finally able to stay awake, his head felt as if it was about to explode and every bone in his body was aching. Skeeter's vision was blurred and pains shot through his midsection when he tried to take a deep breath. Some ribs were broken all right, Beals thought to himself, and no tellin' what else.

Skeeter began to take stock of the situation; he had no idea how long he had been out. Had it been one hour or two, maybe more? They would be coming back, but when? Beals knew he must try to get out of there as soon as he could but wasn't sure if he could even walk, much less having the strength to free himself from the rope.

Beals felt down his leg to the back of his boots. Ah, the idiot left my spurs, he thought with a half-smile that instantly drove pain across his battered face. He grimaced from the pain, but realized he had a chance to free himself by using the rowels on his spurs to gnaw through the rope.

Skeeter crossed his spurs in an effort to hold one of the rowels from turning. He then raked the rope which bound his wrists back and forth over the rowel, hoping it was sharp enough to cut through.

Skeeters' arms began to ache after only a short time, but he continued trying for what seemed forever. His body was telling him to give up, but his mind kept his arms moving the rope up and down on the rowel.

Beals could hardly feel his arms now and was starting to feel dizzy again. He thought he might pass out again when he sensed one of the rope cords was beginning to unravel. Yes, he felt it again. He tried to put just a little more effort into it when suddenly the rope gave way and his hands were free.

Skeeter lay back for a moment, hoping some feeling would come back to his arms. He realized he might not have much time before they would be coming back, how soon, he didn't know. With all the strength he could muster Beals forced himself up on one elbow. He continued fighting to remain conscious. As nausea swept over him he threw up. His head cleared somewhat, so he tried to sit upright and did so with great effort and agony.

For the next ten or fifteen minutes, Skeeter crawled his way toward the now moonlit window, pausing momentarily after each physical exertion to catch his breath and let the pain subside. He finally made it to the window and sat with his back to the wall for a couple of minutes to build up enough strength to pull himself to his feet.

Skeeter positioned his feet in as close as he could so his legs could do most of the work. Using a wooden chair that was directly under the window, he pushed and pulled himself to his feet. He leaned against the wall next to the window, thinking he was going to pass out, but he hung on.

The window was made of four single panes of glass with a frame that hinged on one side, which was a bit of luck for Beals. There was no way he could raise a sliding window, and he didn't want to break the glass for fear the noise might tip off his escape.

The dim light from the window brightened a little, then went back to dim. The sound of thunder rumbled off in the distance. A storm was brewing. The little shack creaked and moaned as the winds shifted with the storm front moving in.

Beals reached to unlatch the window, and with a slight push it swung open. A breeze of cool, fresh, rain-scented air came through the window and wrapped around Skeeter. The fresh air felt good and seemed to help him feel a little stronger.

It is now or never, Beals thought to himself as he lifted his right foot to the seat of the chair. He leaned through the window while trying to put as little weight as possible on his broken ribs. He pushed off the chair with his legs as he leaned forward and fell left shoulder first to the ground just outside of the window. Pain shot through his entire body as his shoulder hit the ground, causing him to lose consciousness again.

Skeeter woke up some fifteen minutes later with raindrops splattering on his face. It wasn't raining hard, just a light shower that felt good. His throat was parched and dry, and he wanted a drink of water badly. He opened his mouth to catch some moisture on his tongue and it helped some.

Beals knew he had to move. His time had to be running out. They would be coming back soon. With his back to the outer wall of the shack, he pushed with his legs and slid up the now rain-soaked boards. His legs were the least damaged of all his body parts, so he was actually more comfortable standing.

Skeeter started moving slowly to the south away for the shack and toward the back of the buildings that ran along the east side of Main Street. The rain was coming down a little harder now, which was in his favor. Since McGlass and the other two hadn't come back to check on him before, they were not likely to get out in this rain to do so now. Besides, they were probably all liquored up by now and thinkin' they'd work on him again tomorrow.

Beals was about to the end of the row of buildings when he saw a large shadowy figure standing at the corner of the last building. He stopped dead in his tracks and reached, out of habit, for his gun that wasn't there.

"Son of a ..." he cursed to himself.

Beals held very still. It was obvious whoever it was had not seen him. Lightning lit the sky, causing the figure to move its head up and down.

"It's a horse!" Beals exclaimed in a whisper. He couldn't believe his luck, and a saddled one to boot. He moved closer. "Well, I'll be damned! It's my old plug. Woo, hoss, woo now," Beals spoke softly to the bay. He caught up the reins and with great effort climbed into the saddle. "Those bastards didn't even take care of my hoss, what a sorry bunch," Beals was thinking this to himself as he headed the bay south out of town for a ways before circling around to the north in the direction of the ranch. The fact that the men neglected his horse seemed to bother Skeeter more than the beating they had given him.

Beals was still in bad shape and had to take it easy because of the pain. He rode slowly in the rain-filled night. He had been beaten badly, but he had also been lucky to get away, lucky to be alive, and he knew it.

Chapter 9

V ANPELT WALKED OUT of the Doc's office where he spent the last hour with Marshal Fossett discussing all that had taken place the last few weeks. VanPelt and Doc Sherman filled the Marshal in on different facts they knew and also their speculations. The Marshal listened and relayed some pieces of the puzzle he knew, which wasn't much. The Marshal had decided to go up to Covington and try to find out who was the main money man behind this land company that was making all those buy-out offers.

Cam stepped into the saddle of the Appaloosa and noticed that Skeeter's' bay was gone from in front of the mercantile as he rode south out of town. Skeeter must have finished picking up the supplies and headed back to the ranch, he thought.

VanPelt did his usual double-back before heading for the ranch. Off to the southwest he could see the clouds starting to build and hoped he would make it back before the rain started.

The Spoonhour ranch was slowly getting back into shape. With Jake doing better, Jenny was not tied down to taking care of him so much, so she was able to do more of the outside chores, which allowed Julio to make rounds and work the cattle.

Jake walked in the front door of the ranch house and slowly sat down in the rocker that was situated where he could see out the front window. The past couple of days Jake had made great progress in regaining his strength back.

"Tenth trip to the barn and back today," Jake stated proudly as Jenny came in from the kitchen with a large glass of freshly made lemonade.

"I'd tell ya not to push it too hard, but you wouldn't listen to me, would ya?" Jenny said in a half-nagging voice as she handed Jake the drink. She knew full well that Jake would push himself to the limit and beyond to get back to his normal strength, which was way above normal for most men. She also knew that not being able to fight his own battle or protect what was his was eating at him.

"I'm doing fine, Jen, don't you worry your pretty head 'bout me. Come back here and give me one of your sugar kisses, this here lemonade ain't quite sweet enough," Jake said with a big grin as he took Jenny's hand and pulled her toward him.

"Uh huh, you ARE feeling better if you're starting to think like that," Jenny teased as she bent down and gave Jake a peck on the cheek.

"I been lifting buckets filled with corn each trip out to the barn to build my arms back up. If my arms weren't plumb give out, I'd show you a trick I learned back in the Civil War," Jake was almost laughing out loud as he finished.

Jenny started to laugh with Jake; she now knew he was going to be just fine. They teased back and forth for awhile when Jenny finally asked, "Be serious now, Jake, what are you planning to do? We can't live in fear of being shot every time we walk outside or when we go into town."

"No, hon, we can't. What we're going to do is find out who's the head honcho that's behind all this land stealing and killing and go after him. Like my old daddy used to say, if you cut a chicken's head off, the body will flop around a bit, but sooner or later it's gonna die," Jake finished.

"What about Corsey and his bunch? Do you think he's the head man?" Jenny asked.

"No, Corsey's not smart enough to plan all this. Will Corsey and his bunch are the body, and in this case we may have to go after the body first," Jake answered.

A low rumble of thunder sounded off in the southwest, and it was beginning to get a little darker outside from the dark clouds that were rolling in. Jenny had gone back into the kitchen to start supper when Jake heard the beat of horse hoofs coming through the front gate. With one glance Jake could tell by the fluid-like movements of the rider it was Cam on the Appaloosa. VanPelt rode with the grace and ease as though the horse and rider were one. Jake greeted Cam with a "door's open!"

"You're lookin' kinda' spry for a half-dead man," Cam said as he flipped his hat on an empty peg by the door.

"He's FEELING kinda' spry for a half-dead man, too," Jenny giggled as she came back in from the kitchen carrying a glass of lemonade for Cam.

VanPelt shared with Jake and Jenny where he and Skeeter had been that day. He started with what they had seen and the signs they found that told pretty much the story of what had happened at the Howard Reed place. He went on to explain the weird demise of Dave Kinsel and finished with the visit he had had with Marshal Fossett and Doc Sherman.

"Speakin' of Skeeter, I thought he would have already been here. I figured he left town 'bout an hour before I did," Cam said as he stroked his chin.

"Haven't seen him since you two pulled out this morning," Jake returned.

Jenny could tell by the expressions of both men that they were suddenly concerned.

"Maybe he stopped off somewhere on the way, maybe for a drink or something," Jenny found herself not believing what she was saying as she said it.

"I'd think Skeeter would try to get back here as soon as he could with the look of rain and all," Cam continued as he looked outside. "It's starting to spit a little now. I think before I put the App up for the night, I'll ride to our camp up on the hill and check to see if he stopped off there. Be back in a minute," he said as he grabbed his hat and went out the door.

At the camp, Cam found no signs off anyone being there since they had left that morning. VanPelt was beginning to really worry now. He knew that Skeeter was no green horn and was aware of how severe storms in the Oklahoma Territory could be.

Cam reined in the Appaloosa and stepped down in front of the barn just as the rain started to pour. He opened the barn door and led his horse to one of the empty stalls. The thunder and lighting was making the App nervous, but after peeling the saddle from the animal's back and removing his bridle, Cam give him a thorough rubdown. This calmed the big spotted horse, and soon he was chomping away on some oats Cam had poured into the feed bin and didn't seem to care about anything else. VanPelt forked some hay into the stall as well and headed for the house.

The rain was coming down in buckets now, and VanPelt was soaked by the time he got to the front porch. Jenny met him at the door with a towel to dry off with and stood in the doorway, not letting him pass, until he had taken off his now mud-caked boots.

Jenny held the screen door open for Cam after the boots were off, and they both went inside.

"Skeeter's not up there at the camp either and no signs showin' he had been there," Cam reported.

"Not good, what do ya think?" Jake asked.

"One of two things, he didn't leave town when I thought he did, and now he's held up somewhere waitin' for this storm to blow over or he's run into some trouble," Cam offered with a serious tone.

"What do you mean trouble, what kind of trouble?" Jenny asked with her eyes wide with concern.

"Oh, Jenny, you know Skeeter. His mouth was always getting him butt-deep into alligators. Why, you remember the time when he was chasin' after that Rader gal back home? I think he must have caught her, too, 'cause her dad and four brothers came lookin' for Skeeter with shotguns and matrimony on their minds," Jake was reminiscing, mainly to ease the worry he could see in Jenny's face.

"Didn't that Rader gal end up marryin' some dang lawyer, a Karstetter or somethin' like that?" Cam asked. He knew what Jake was doing and fell right into step with him.

"That's the guy, Karstetter. If it weren't for him, Skeeter would be a married man today and livin' somewhere up in Kansas, of all places," Jake chuckled.

"Okay, you two, supper will be ready in ten minutes," Jenny said, shaking her head as she walked into the kitchen.

No one had much to say during supper. Cam, Jake and Jenny were pretty much wrapped in their own thoughts about where Skeeter might be. The men had pushed back from the table still sipping their coffee while Jenny was removing the dirty dishes, when they heard a couple of horses nicker out by the barn. There was a pole corral with a lean-to off the barn where the spare horses were kept. A horse is as good as a watchdog if a person pays attention to what the horse is tryin' to tell ya.

VanPelt was up in an instant, staying low until he was out the front door. Jake was not far behind after taking up his rifle and snuffing the lamp that was lighting the parlor.

Jenny did the same with the lamp in the kitchen and grabbed up another rifle she kept by the wash basin and dropped to one knee just inside the back door.

Cam and Jake were at the corner of the house but still on the front porch when a flash of lightning lit the sky. It was just enough light for them to make out the silhouette of a horse with its rider slumped over in the saddle.

"Skeeter," Jake yelled.

Leaping off the porch, Cam and Jake headed on a dead run toward the horse and rider. "Damn," Cam said when he realized he was sloshing through the mud in his socking feet. Both men slowed to a walk and started speaking softly to the horse as they got near, not wanting to spook him.

"It's Skeeter all right, and he's looked better," Cam said.

"Hold on to him while I lead his horse to the front porch. He'll be more comfortable in the house than in the barn," Jake instructed as he took hold of the bridle.

At the porch Cam pulled Skeeter from the saddle and carried him into the house, while Jake led Skeeter's bay back to the barn where he tended to him before heading to the house.

By the time Jake came back from the barn, Cam had taken Skeeter up to the loft, as per Jenny's instructions, and was getting him out of his blood and water-soaked clothes. Jenny had started a fire in the fireplace to heat a pot of water and was tearing an old bed sheet for bandages.

Skeeter was fading in and out of conscience and was kind of delirious.

"Who did this to ya, buddy, can you hear me, huh, can you hear what I'm sayin', who did this to ya?" Cam was saying as Jake came upstairs.

Skeeter had passed out again when Jenny came up with a wash bowl of warm water and towels to clean his wounds. He was in bad shape, that was for sure, but at least they couldn't find any gunshot or knife wounds.

After cleaning and bandaging all of Skeeter's wounds and agreeing that he was resting quietly, Cam, Jake and Jenny pulled chairs up in front of the fireplace. In late August in the Oklahoma Territory, a rainstorm sometimes cools things down a bit, giving a warning of weather to come, and the fire felt good.

The three friends sat staring into the fire as they were deep in their own thoughts. A drop of moisture oozed out of the end of a log dropped down and sizzled away to nothing.

"Time we take it to 'um, Jake," Cam said with his jaw mussels twitching.

"It's time," Jake answered.

Chapter 10

THE NEXT MORNING Skeeter was a little better but was pretty weak from all the blood he had lost. He was at least able to give a sketchy account of what had happened to him.

"Man, that McKay packs a wallop! I thought I'd been kicked with the north end of a southbound mule," Beals exclaimed.

"Skeeter, did you pick up on anything that might tell us who those hombres are workin' for?" Jake asked while pulling at his chin.

"No, can't think of anything they said. 'Course, I'm not thinkin' too straight right now. Maybe something'll come to me later," Skeeter answered.

"So we still don't know who the money man is. Sure would like to know the answer to that before we go after that bunch," Jake said, thinking out loud.

"Hey, you ain't takin' out after those no-good skunks without me, are ya? I want a piece of that Enos character for myself. Dang coward is pretty tough when he's got the drop on ya." Skeeter started coughing halfway through his sentence. "I'll be good as new in a couple of days."

"Okay, time to let Skeeter rest, everyone out of here," Jenny stepped in and tried to push Jake and Cam toward the stairs.

"We'll hold off for a few days. We wouldn't want you to miss out on this one," Jake said to Skeeter.

Skeeter cracked a half-smile with a slight nod as he lay back and closed his eyes.

When Jake came down the stairs, he saw VanPelt pulling his boots on and seemed to be in a hurry. He looked up at Jake, who had a puzzled look on his face.

"I'm going to make a run up to Covington. Maybe Marshal Fossett has dug up something on who's been buyin' up all the land." Cam answered Jake's question before he asked it. "I'll do my best to make it back in a day or two."

Jake just nodded as if to say good idea and said, "I'll get Jenny to bag you a little somethin' to eat on the way."

VanPelt went to the barn to saddle the Appaloosa. The morning after the storm was crisp and clean. VanPelt gave the Appaloosa a bit of oats to eat while Cam packed his bed roll. He loved this time of year when the mornings and evenings were cool and clear. In another week or two the trees would begin to turn, and that was his favorite. Add the different colors of the trees to an Oklahoma sunset and a body could have a preview of what heaven will be like.

VanPelt covered the eight or nine miles north to Covington in a little less than three hours. The rain water from last night's storm had caused most of the creeks to crest over their banks and made it more difficult for Cam to travel the low ground. He even had to back-track a couple of times to find a better place to cross one of the tributaries of Black Bear Creek which was normally dry this time of year, but after the heavy rain was running deep and swift. This tributary ran somewhat west to east about two miles south of Covington and connected to Black Bear Creek about a mile and a half east of town. Black Bear Creek ran from the northwest to the southeast on the northeast side of Covington.

VanPelt entered town from the east. Covington was laid out much like most small towns that now dotted the landscape after the run of '89. Its main street ran east to west, mainly to slow down the prevailing wind from the south, as well as the cold north winds in the winter.

Covington was a somewhat larger town than Marshall with another street, Jefferson Street, which also ran east and west one block north of Main Street. Connecting these two streets, at the east end of town, was Noble Street. A very large livery stable and blacksmith shop was situated on the northeast corner of Main and Noble with an equally large group of corrals or holding pens constructed behind the stables. The holding pens were mostly empty except for a half-dozen old mustangs that looked to be waiting for the glue factory.

Cam tied the Appaloosa on the west side of the livery to a hitching post which had a watering trough positioned beneath it. A gunshot echoed from down the street. Then another, and then a third shot rang out.

Cam ducked inside the livery and peered through a slightly opened door. Four men with guns drawn ran out of the First Bank of Covington which was halfway down the block on the south side of Main Street.

A fifth man was mounted and holding reins of the horses for the other four men.

One of the four coming out of the bank shot twice more through the bank's door before swinging into the saddle, and with the rest of his compadres headed west out of town on a full run.

Cam ran down the street to the front of the bank and arrived there at the same time as Marshal Bill Forrest. A man with bloodstains all over the front of his shirt staggered out of the bank door. The man was pointing in the direction where the bandits had gone as he gasped, "Cherokee Bill, it was Cherokee Bill and his gang."

Crawford Goldsby (a.k.a. Cherokee Bill) was born at Fort Concho, Texas, on February 8, 1876. It was said Bill was of African, European and Indian ancestry.

When Cherokee Bill was twelve, he killed his first man, his brother-in-law. Story has it when his brother-in law told him to go feed the hogs, Bill turned with a gun he had been cleaning and killed him. Cherokee Bill was not prosecuted for this killing because of his young age. A few years later, Goldsby fell in with William and James Cook. The Cook brothers were two of the worst outlaws in the Indian Nations.

Goldsby was given the nickname "Cherokee Bill" by William Cook. Bill was riding with the Cook brothers when a posse cornered the three desperadoes near Tahlequah, Indian Territory, in June of 1894. The lawmen had a warrant for the arrest of James Cook on a charge of larceny, but when they moved in to make the arrest, all three youths went for their guns. The outlaws were able to drive the lawmen back and made a run for it, with the posse hot on their heels. As they were being chased, Cherokee Bill turned in his saddle and fired a shot that killed Deputy Sequoyah Houston. Now, at the age of eighteen, Bill was a wanted man on the run.

Marshal Fossett sent one of his deputies, W.C. Smith, to organize a posse to chase after the bandits before he went into the bank to check out the damage. He asked VanPelt to accompany him inside.

As they entered, the bank was in chaos. Two women were huddled in one corner crying, a man lay face down a few feet away from the women and had a bloody wound on the side of his head. Behind the teller's cage another man was moaning and holding his arm. He, too, had been shot, but it didn't look serious.

Marshal Fossett walked around behind the teller cage and checked the wounded arm of Tom Harms, the bank president and a good friend of the marshal.

"Are you all right, Tom?" the Marshal asked.

"I'll be okay," Tom replied with a grimace. "He didn't have to shoot. We were giving him the money. He just started shooting for no reason and looked like he enjoyed doing it."

"Tom, was it Cherokee Bill like Jim was saying out front?" Fossett asked.

"Cherokee Bill, sure enough," Harms continued. "He yelled, 'This is the Cherokee Bill Gang and we're robbin' this here bank.' That scum wanted us to know who was robbing us ... never seen anything like it."

Deputy Marshal Smith entered the bank and told Fossett he had ten men sworn in and ready to ride.

Marshal Fossett turned to VanPelt.

"You want to join us?" the Marshal asked, "I'll fill you in on the latest I know about the Oklahoma Land Company as we ride," he continued.

"I'll get my horse," Cam said. And with that he was out the bank door heading for the livery stable.

Chapter 11

THE POSSE PICKED up the trail of the bank robbers at the edge of Covington. With the ground still wet from the recent rain, it was an easy trail to follow. The trail turned due north about a half-mile west of town.

As they rode, Marshal Fossett related to VanPelt the details he had uncovered about the "Oklahoma Land Company." It seems that most of the land transactions were handled by different land companies and different buyers: the Enid Land Company, the Territory Land Company or the Western Land Company, to name a few. Each different land company would then funnel their holdings back through the "*Oklahoma Land Company.*"

While Fossett was digging through all the paperwork at the Oklahoma Territory Recorder of Deeds in Enid, one name always came up in connection with each land company, and that name was Lester M. Hoch. "The Oklahoma Land Company" is owned by Lester M. Hoch.

"Any connection between Hoch and Corsey's bunch?" Cam asked the Marshal when he had finished.

"I have reports of Corsey being seen with Hoch over around the Enid area, but no one has ever seen them together in Covington or Marshall for that matter," Fossett answered. "I'd bet a dollar to a donut Corsey and his bunch are Hoch's hired guns," Fossett continued.

"I think you would have a safe bet," VanPelt agreed as the tracks the posse had been following came upon Black Bear Creek. The creek was fairly wide at this point, which allowed for a much shallower crossing.

The posse crossed over and to their expectations no tracks were found on the other side. The outlaws had ridden into the creek and stayed in it going one direction or the other in an effort to lose their pursuers. It worked.

The posse split up into four groups with a group following each side of the creek in both directions. Whichever group found where the bandits tracks came out of the creek were to fire one shot to signal the rest of the posse the trail had been picked back up.

Cam was with the group that went back across the creek and turned to the west, scouting for tracks along the south side of the creek. The Marshal and his group crossed back over the creek and went east.

The group VanPelt went with had traveled about a half-mile when they found the now familiar tracks of the holdup men. The signal was given, and after about fifteen minutes the rest of the posse joined back up, and they continued following the tracks which now led off in a southwesterly direction.

The posse was able to follow the trail of Cherokee Bill and his gang at a fairly fast pace for two more hours before nightfall. Marshal Fossett made the decision to make camp and get an early start at first light.

Daybreak came with another cool crisp morning. Most of the posse awoke to the smell of coffee boiling and bacon frying. Marshal Fossett didn't sleep much during the night, so he had breakfast going so the men could get an early start. After each man had at least one cup of strong black coffee with bacon and some hard tack, they were in the saddle again. The trail was still clear as the posse followed it to the outskirts of Waukomis, a small town about eight miles south of Enid.

When the posse rode in, the town was all a-buzz. It seems Cherokee Bill and his gang had just robbed the general store. The bandits took ammunition, food and what little money the store keeper had in his till.

"These hombres have more nerve than sense." Marshal Fossett said in disgust as the local sheriff was approaching.

The local sheriff, Lawrence Powell, had worked with Fossett as railroad detectives out of Atchison, Kansas, a couple of years back, and they had great respect for each other.

Sheriff Powell related to Marshal Fossett the details about the robbery that had just taken place. It seems the store robbery went much like the bank holdup — the store clerk was cooperating as did the people in the bank — but Cherokee Bill shot him anyway. Sheriff Powell went on to say the storekeeper was just wounded in the shoulder and should be okay.

Fossett told Powell the reason he and his posse were hot on the bandits' trail and thought it best they keep moving.

"Looks like we've made up some ground on those hombres,"

Fossett stated. "We can't be more than thirty minutes or so behind them."

"We'll be back through to let you know what happened, and you can buy me a beer for old times," Fossett said as he tugged at the brim of his hat and nodded his head to Sheriff Powell.

The posse headed west out of Waukomis, and at the edge of town, they picked up the outlaws' trail again. The trail headed in a westerly direction toward either Drummond or Ames.

The posse picked up their pace in the hopes of catching up to Cherokee Bill and his gang before they reached another town.

About five miles west of Waukomis the trail led the posse to the east bank of Turkey Creek. The creek was only twenty to thirty yards wide, not very deep, and was tree-lined with a large wooded area on the opposite side. It appeared the outlaws had crossed the creek at this point.

"Marshal, I don't like the looks of this," VanPelt spoke softly.

"You could be right, everyone dismount," Fossett ordered.

As Fossett leaned over and swung his leg around and down, a bullet ricocheted off a limb just above his head. Then, all hell broke loose with a hail of gunfire coming from the trees on the west side of the creek.

The posse had scattered for cover with the sound of the first shot and was now returning fire in the direction the shooting came from.

There were a number of dead falls on the east side of the creek, which gave good cover, and by outnumbering the outlaws four to one, the posse poured lead into the area where the outlaws were shooting from.

After return fire had stopped, Marshal Fossett gave the signal to cease fire. All was quiet for about ten minutes.

Fossett looked around for VanPelt and spotted him off to his right. VanPelt was on the move, but he stayed low behind a bush-covered sandy ridge that ran to the north about ten yards back from the creek.

The Marshal passed the word that VanPelt was working his way around behind the bandits and to hold fire so as not to hit him.

VanPelt slipped into the creek water without making a ripple. He was about a hundred yards north of where the posse was and swam underwater to the opposite bank. Without a sound, he worked his way back south toward the outlaws.

Still staying low and with the cover of trees, VanPelt moved to within twenty-five feet behind the bandits. There were three men, but only one of them was holding a rifle. The other two were lying face down in pools of their own blood.

"Move and you're a dead man. Now drop the rifle and reach," VanPelt spoke slow and evenly.

The man flinched but froze immediately. He then complied with VanPelt's order and dropped his rifle.

Still remaining behind a tree, VanPelt spoke again. "Now unbuckle your gun belt and let it drop."

"Don't shoot me, mister, I give up," the man said as he did what he was told.

"Turn around but don't stand up. Not knowing you're not armed, my friends may put a hole in ya," VanPelt said.

The man followed VanPelt's orders, and as he turned VanPelt, with a disgusted expression on his face, asked, "How old are you, kid?"

Hanging his head, "Fourteen, sir," he answered with an ashamed whimper.

VanPelt yelled to the Marshal that all was clear. After getting a response back, he walked over and picked up the young man's guns. He then checked the other men and found them to be dead. Neither of the two men was much older than their sidekick, maybe seventeen or eighteen years old.

Marshal Fossett and most of the posse had crossed the creek and rode up to find VanPelt sitting cross-legged in front of his captive.

VanPelt stood and walked over to the Marshal Fossett. Pushing his hat back on his head, he said, "According to this kid, Cherokee Bill told him and the other two to stay put and wait to ambush us as we crossed the creek. Bill told these three kids if they didn't do what he said he would come back and kill them himself. I guess the kid was more scared of Cherokee Bill than he was of us. The kid also said the other man riding with Bill is James Cook, one of the Cook brothers. They've got about an hour's head start on us."

The Marshal talked the situation over with the rest of the posse, most of whom had jobs back in Covington to get back to. The decision was made to take the two bodies and the kid back to Waukomis. The Marshal would send out wanted posters on Cherokee Bill and

James Cook with their latest crimes listed and hope to get information back as to their whereabouts.

VanPelt mounted his horse, which the Marshal had brought from the other side of the creek, and said, "Marshal, if you don't need me any more, I'll be heading back to the Spoonhour Ranch and fill them in on what you have told me about Lester Hoch. I want you to know, we'll be going after Will Corsey and his bunch for what they did to Jake," he finished.

"I'll be in Marshall in two days. Can you hold off doing anything until I get there?" Fossett asked. "And I'll arrest Hoch at that time."

"This is Wednesday, we'll be in town at noon on Friday. Will that give you enough time?" VanPelt asked.

"Friday at noon it is, but try not to open the ball until you hear from me," Fossett instructed.

VanPelt pulled at his hat as he nodded his head, then reined the Appaloosa around and headed back across Turkey Creek.

Chapter 12

JAKE SPOONHOUR and Camron VanPelt walked their horses slowly down Main Street of Marshall, followed closely behind by Skeeter Beals and Jenny Spoonhour. The four reined up in front of Shotgun Sam's Saloon before anyone took notice of them and realized who they were.

As they dismounted, an elderly man sitting on the wooden bench that was positioned beneath the left front window of the saloon glanced up from the stick of wood he was whittling on and then looked back down. His head snapped back up with his eyes wide open and nearly swallowed his plug of tobacco.

"Mr. Spoonhour?" the old-timer mouthed the name in a gasping whisper as he came to his feet and then scurried up the boardwalk faster than he had moved in years. He ran into a man and lady coming from the other direction and nearly knocked them over. He looked back and pointed at Jake as he said, "Jake Spoonhour, that's Jake Spoonhour," and was off again to tell someone else.

The lady caught her breath, and the man did a double-take as they both realized it was indeed Jake Spoonhour rose from the dead. The two stumbled off the boardwalk together and crossed the street, narrowly being missed by a speeding team of horses pulling a buckboard. The driver had just heard the news and was gawking, with his mouth open at Jake and not paying attention to what he was doing.

"You better get off the street before the sight of you gets someone hurt," Jenny commented, half-kidding and half not.

Jake looked over the batwings and peered into the smoke-filled saloon. Will Corsey was bellied up to the bar about midway down with his back to the front door. To his right stood Jim Enos, laughing loudly while pawing one of the working ladies.

"Watch your backs, I don't see McGlass or McKay," Jake said in a low voice as he went through the batwings.

All four entered the room as one. VanPelt moved off to the left end of the bar. Beals walked down the wall to the far right side of the room, close to the back door. Jenny stepped to her left just inside the front door, keeping her scattergun at her side half-hidden with her riding skirt as she leaned cautiously against the wall.

Jake quickly moved to the bar and stood right beside Corsey. Corsey was caught up in his own thoughts and noticed nothing until a deadly silence spread over the room. It seemed as if everyone in the room, except Corsey and Enos, saw Jake Spoonhour at the same time. The only sound heard was the idiot Enos still laughing.

Corsey looked up into the mirror behind the bar and went cold. He turned to his left toward Jake and drew his Colt with his right hand all in one motion. He made a low moaning sound from deep down in his throat that seemed to build as he turned.

As Corsey's gun came up, Jake grabbed it with his bare left hand and clamped down tight over the already cocked hammer, preventing the gun from firing. Jake pushed down and twisted the gun along with Corsey's hand at the same time. Corsey screamed with pain as the bones in his wrist snapped causing him to release his grip on the Colt. Jake eased the hammer down on the gun after snatching it from Corsey's hand and tossed it toward the front door.

By this time, Enos had figured out that this was no place for a coward such as himself. He slowly started backing toward the back door. As he neared the door, he bumped into someone and then felt the cold steel of a gun barrel beneath his right ear.

"Now ain't this a switch?" Beals said softly and very slowly.

Enos wet himself right then and there.

"You wouldn't want to miss any of this fun now, would ya? Oh, you would? Well, all right, just back real slow-like out this here door," instructed Beals. The door closed, and a few seconds later Beals came back in with a big smile. He looked across the room at VanPelt and gave him a nod and a wink.

Corsey was insane with rage. In the past, if he didn't think he could take a man with his bare hands or didn't want to work up a sweat, he would simply gun them down. Corsey started throwing punches as hard and fast as he could at Jake. In his rage, Corsey didn't feel the pain of his wrist or realize that his hand was flopping limply on the end of his arm.

Jake sidestepped the barrage of punches and came in low with a left uppercut to the mid-section that lifted Corsey off his feet. Jake let

Corsey straighten himself up and then let go with a solid right that shook Bad Bill to his heels. Jake came with another right, but this one was with all the strength he had. This one was for all the settlers Corsey and his bunch had killed or driven from their homes, but mainly this one was for nearly making Jenny a widow.

Jake brought this punch almost from the floor, and when it landed, Corsey's face literally exploded with blood flying everywhere. Corsey dropped in a heap on the saloon floor.

The saloon was still without a sound. Everyone was in a trance-like state, not believing what they just saw.

"How 'bout a beer, Sam?" VanPelt broke the silence.

"What? Oh sure, be right there," Sam said as he came back to reality.

That brought everybody back to life as they began to relive the fight with each other like they weren't even there. Some came up and slapped Jake on the back, telling him how glad they were to see him.

Jake looked over to where Jenny was standing by the front door and gave her a wink. Jenny made out like she was yawning, but then gave him a big smile and winked back.

Skeeter had gone out the back door and was bringing the half-conscious Enos in. Enos had a stream of blood trickling down the side of his head from where Skeeter had given Mr. Enos a little payback. Beals shoved Enos to the floor beside Corsey and ordered a beer.

Jenny had been watching a man who had been sitting on the far right side of the saloon. It appeared to her that this man was trying very hard to be inconspicuous. He was now nervously heading toward the door while staying as close to the front wall and as far away from Jake as he could. As he reached the batwings, Jenny spoke to him.

"Are you Mr. Hoch, Mr. Lester Hoch?" she asked.

Hoch was startled at first, but seeing the inquiry came from a very pretty lady, he answered. "Why, yes, yes, I am, and to whom do I owe this honor?"

"To the wife of the man you tried to have killed," Jenny answered, and as she spoke she hit Hoch with a very good right cross to the nose. Lester Hoch dropped like a rock and lay there on the floor colder than a frog.

The room fell silent once again as all eyes turned to Hoch and then to Jenny.

"Problem, hon?" Jake asked.

"No, no problem at all," Jenny answered as the batwings opened and Marshal Fossett walked in the room.

The Marshal stopped just inside the doors and pushed his black hat to the back of his head as he surveyed the room. He then stepped across Hoch's unconscious body and walked over to where Jake was standing.

"I thought you were going to wait until I got here to make your move?" Marshal Fossett asked Jake as he bent down and checked Corsey for signs of life. "Looks like he's going to live long enough to get hung," the Marshal continued.

"We stirred up too much of a commotion as we rode into town. It seems people don't get to see a dead man ridin' down the street every day. We figured if we waited, we might lose the element of surprise," Jake answered with a half-smile.

"I caught Pat McGlass saddling his horse at the livery when I first came into town. He was in one almighty hurry to light a shuck out of here. I put him up over to the jail, and I reckon that'll be a good place for these three as well. I'll have Doc check 'em over after they're locked up," Marshal said, with the last part as an afterthought.

Right then, the batwing door flew open and a young boy of about 12 years old burst into the room all wide-eyed and talking excited gibberish.

"Slow down, boy. What's the problem?" Marshal Fossett asked as he grabbed the boy by both shoulders.

"That man, he said to send the Injun-lookin' feller out. He said he's a waitin' in the street fir him," the boy answered as he pointed toward the street.

"What man, who sent ya in here?" Fossett prodded.

Jenny had pushed open the batwings just enough to look out and there standing in the middle of the street was Tom McKay, looking bigger and meaner than any man she had ever seen before.

Jenny turned back to speak to the Marshal and looked at Jake, then to VanPelt. "It's McKay," was all she said.

VanPelt's expression didn't change. He lifted the mug of beer to his lips and drank the remainder down. All eyes were glued on him as he pushed away from the bar and started for the door.

"Son, you don't have to do this. I'll deputize a half-dozen of these gents and we'll go arrest that no-good hombre," Marshal Fossett said as he caught VanPelt by the elbow.

"He's got it to do, Marshal, let him go," Jake said flatly.

VanPelt continued toward the door, and as he neared Jenny, he raised one eyebrow on an otherwise solemn face. He stopped at the door and looked outside to see McKay standing in the middle of the street with his legs spread slightly and his right hand hovering over a Colt revolver. The huge man was a menacing sight just standing there, towering above the dusty street. He made all things around him look small; even the horses that stood at a nearby hitching post looked smaller compared to McKay.

Someone over by the bar cleared his throat, and that was the only sound that came from the twenty-some odd people still in the room. Jenny had placed her hand on VanPelt's arm and parted her lips to speak, but there was nothing to say. Jenny's hand slid from his arm as Cam pushed through the doors and stepped out onto the boardwalk.

" 'Bout time, Injun, I was beginnin' to think you was yella'," McKay growled as people scurried about trying to find the best vantage point to watch what was about to take place. Their main concern was a spot with a good view, but one that was out of the line of fire.

"Word's out that you're pretty fast with a gun, is that right? Word also has it that you may be faster than me," McKay barked.

VanPelt stepped off the boardwalk and into the street, but said nothing as he slowly walked to the center of the street. His eyes were cold and dark as he kept them fixed on McKay's every move. When VanPelt was about twenty paces from McKay, he stopped and turned to face the big man.

"I'm fixin' to answer all them questions 'cause there ain't nobody faster than me, specially some dirty Injun," McKay continued his taunting.

VanPelt's expression still never changed, and he still said nothing. It was like he was bored or something. Like maybe, McKay was taking up VanPelt's time, time he didn't want to waste.

McKay finally shut up and stared into VanPelt's eyes and for a brief instant thought this might not be such a good idea. The feeling passed as quickly as it came, and Tom McKay reached for his gun.

VanPelt's hand was a blur as his Colt leaped to life and spoke its reverberating report.

McKay had a very puzzled look on his face, a look of disbelief. He also had a small round dot, which was beginning to trickle blood located just above the bridge of his nose. McKay's Colt was in his hand, suspended halfway out of its holster.

If McKay had a thought, it would have been, "Beals was right, he put a bullet between my eyes before I ever cleared leather."

McKay fell forward face down with violent collision with the dusty street. Some folks later said they could feel the ground shake when he hit.

Jake, Jenny and Skeeter were already in the saddle when VanPelt walked over to where their horses were tied. Cam mounted up without a word from his three friends.

The Marshal Fossett was standing on the boardwalk and spoke, "VanPelt, I got a badge that needs a shirt to hang on, if'n you're lookin' for steady work. There's a race war going on against the Indians down around the Shawnee area."

VanPelt smiled and said, "You people got too many rules." He hesitated, "But I'll keep it in mind."

With that the four reined their horses around and headed out of town.

Chapter 13

No ONE HAD said a word all the way back to the ranch, each handling the day's events in his or her own way.

Jenny went on into the house to start preparing supper, and the others took the horses to the barn.

As they were tending to the horses, VanPelt finally spoke, "Jake, you got a bottle of whiskey in the house?"

"Shore do, do ya need a drink?" Jake asked.

"Yep, maybe two or three," Cam said with a smile as he looked over at Jake. Jake returned the smile with a little chuckle.

"Now we're talkin' my language," Skeeter said and started laughing out loud. "Did you see the look on old Jim Enos' face when I stepped up behind him? I'm a-tellin' ya, that was worth every broken rib they gave me just to see that look," Skeeter laughed some more.

Julio came through the barn door about that time questioning why everyone was so happy.

"Julio, did you ever see anyone so scared that they wet themselves right there on the spot?" Skeeter asked.

"Yes Señor, when those Indians had me before Señor Jake found me," Julio answered. "And I did not think it was so funny."

Everyone was laughing now, except Julio and Beals were rolling on the hay that covered the floor in hysterics.

Jake began to smell food cooking from Jenny's kitchen and said, "What do ya say we have a bit to eat before we uncork that bottle? You, too, Julio," and with that they all headed for the house.

The next morning, everyone was up with the sun. There was a lot of work to catch up on. At the breakfast table Cam told Jake and Jenny that he had decided to take Marshal Fossett up on his job offer and head down to Shawnee.

"Cam, mind if I ride along with ya?" asked Skeeter. "I ain't ever seen that part of the territory."

"You're welcome to come along, but if you get yourself into trouble with some woman, you're on your own," VanPelt said dryly. "And don't call me Cam."

THE END